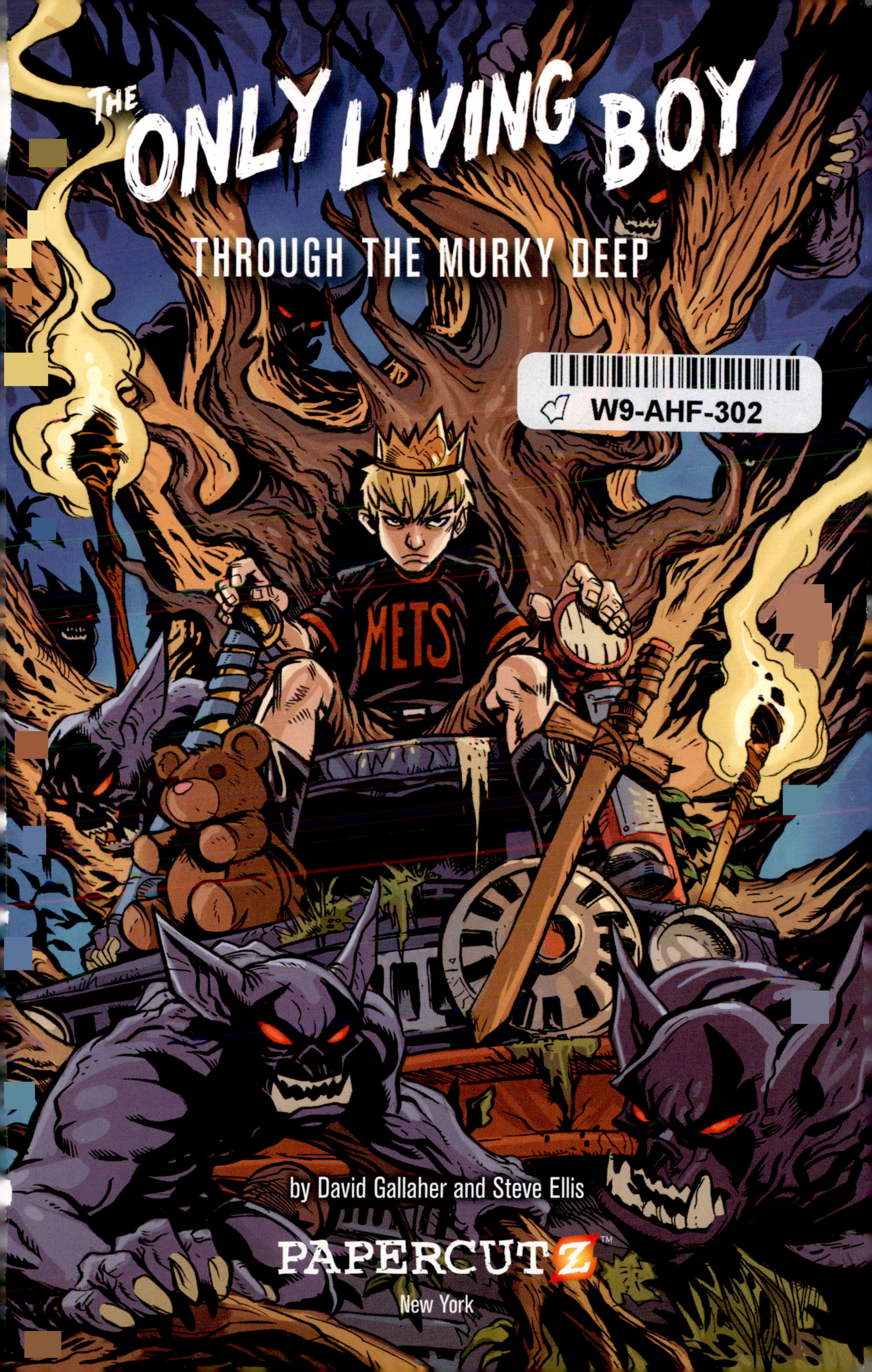
THE ONLY LIVING BOY
THROUGH THE MURKY DEEP
METS
by David Gallaher and Steve Ellis
PAPERCUTZ™
New York

To Drew, Ben and Daniel for being the greatest brothers – David

To Jacob and Luna and to exploring life's greatest adventures – Steve

THE ONLY LIVING BOY #4 "Through the Murky Deep"

Chapters 7 & 8
Writer / Co-Creator: David Gallaher
Artist / Co-Creator: Steve Ellis
Color Flatting: Holley McKend
Lettering: Melanie Ujimori
Consulting Editor: Janelle Asselin
Production Assistance: Allison Strejlau
Assistants: Emily Walton, Luke D. Blackwood

Special Thanks to Dara Hyde

Originally serialized at: www.the-only-living-boy.com

Production – Dawn Guzzo
Cover Logo – Adam Grano
Production Coordinator – Sasha Kimiatek
Assistant Managing Editor - Jeff Whitman
Jim Salicrup
Editor-in-Chief

PB ISBN: 978-1-62991-634-7
HC ISBN: 978-1-62991-635-4

Printed in China. April 2017

Distributed by Macmillan
First Papercutz Printing

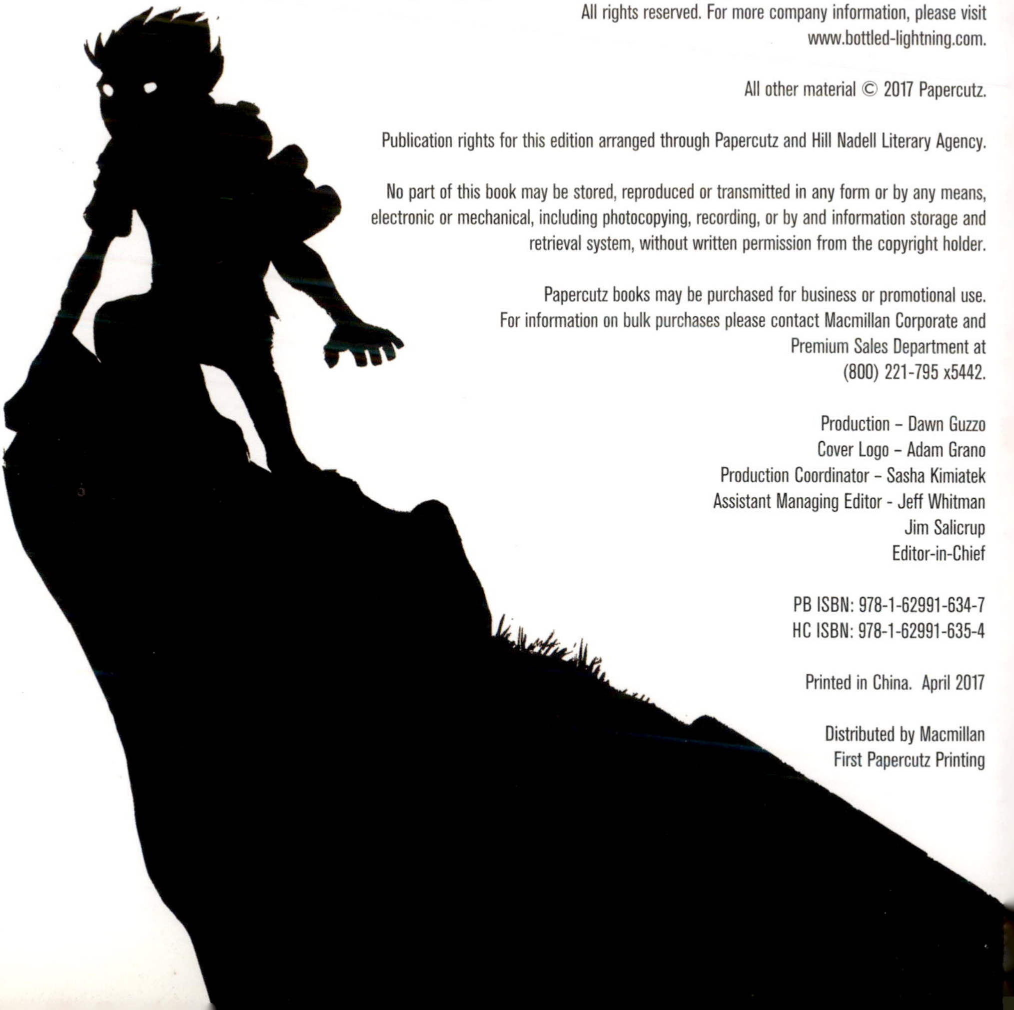

CHAPTER SEVEN

Previously in...

THE ONLY LIVING BOY

After an epic battle at the Hive City of Sectuarius, Erik finds himself at the mercy of Doctor Once and Baalikar. While captured, Erik learns that the creatures he freed from the Census have all been re-captured and subjected to horrible experiments. When he tries to confront Doctor Once, Erik soon finds himself the victim of cruel experiments that reveal his tragic past of loss, loneliness, and death. After fighting back, Erik was able to force Doctor Once to reveal his own path of heartbreak that led the fiendish scientist to create Baalikar and the Patchwork Planet. Fatally wounded from his own machines, with his dying breath, Doctor Once begs Erik to travel North, far beyond the reach of Baalikar's watch. After freeing the rest of the creatures, Erik runs into the woods seeking shelter, where he finds a handmade doll made by the savage Alku. Raising the doll to the sky in a fit of rage, Erik may have just gotten more than he bargained for.

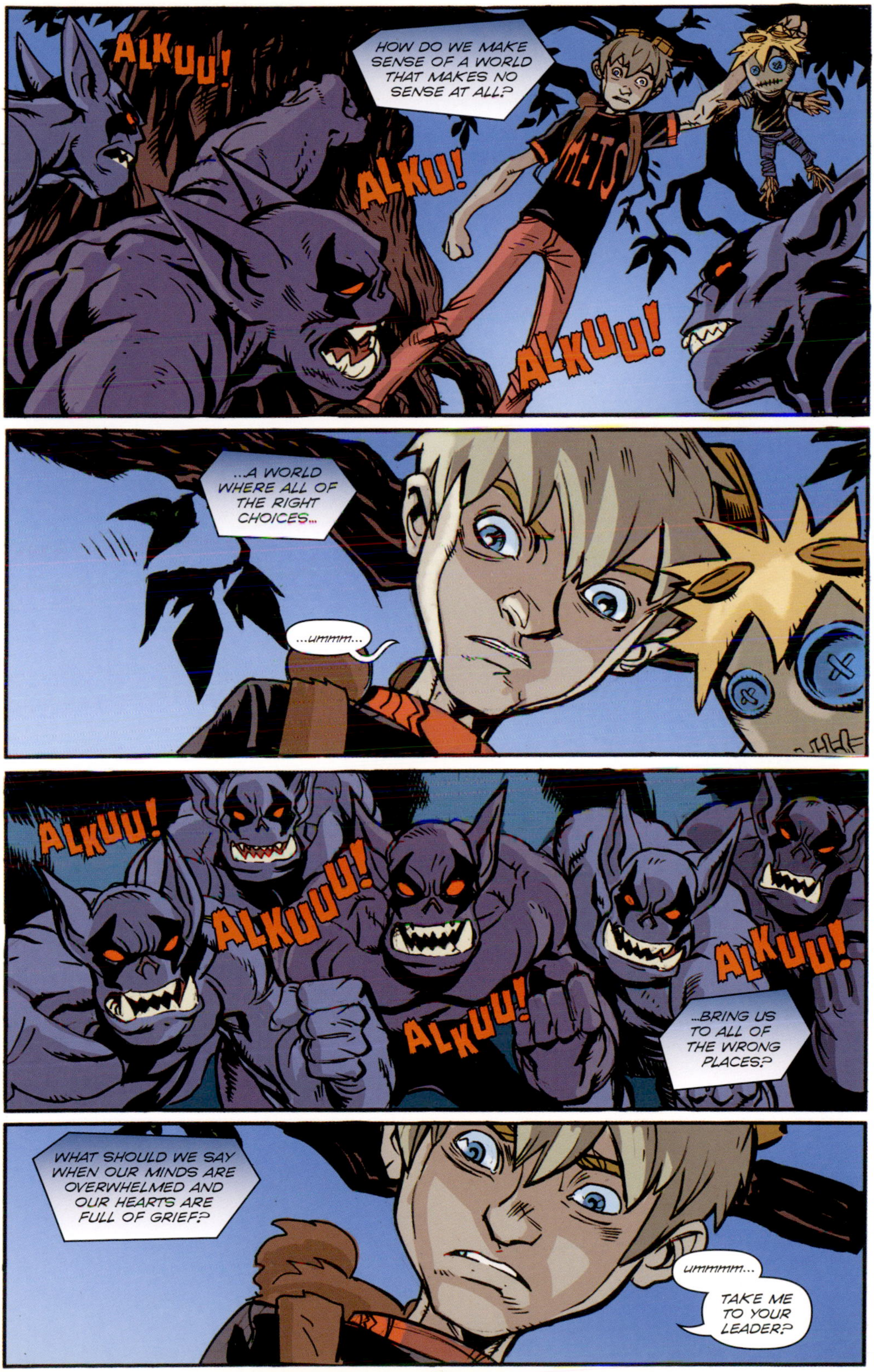
ALKUU!
HOW DO WE MAKE SENSE OF A WORLD THAT MAKES NO SENSE AT ALL?
ALKU!
ALKUU!
...A WORLD WHERE ALL OF THE RIGHT CHOICES...
...ummm...
ALKUU!
ALKUUU!
ALKUU!
ALKUU!
...BRING US TO ALL OF THE WRONG PLACES?
WHAT SHOULD WE SAY WHEN OUR MINDS ARE OVERWHELMED AND OUR HEARTS ARE FULL OF GRIEF?
ummmm...
TAKE ME TO YOUR LEADER?

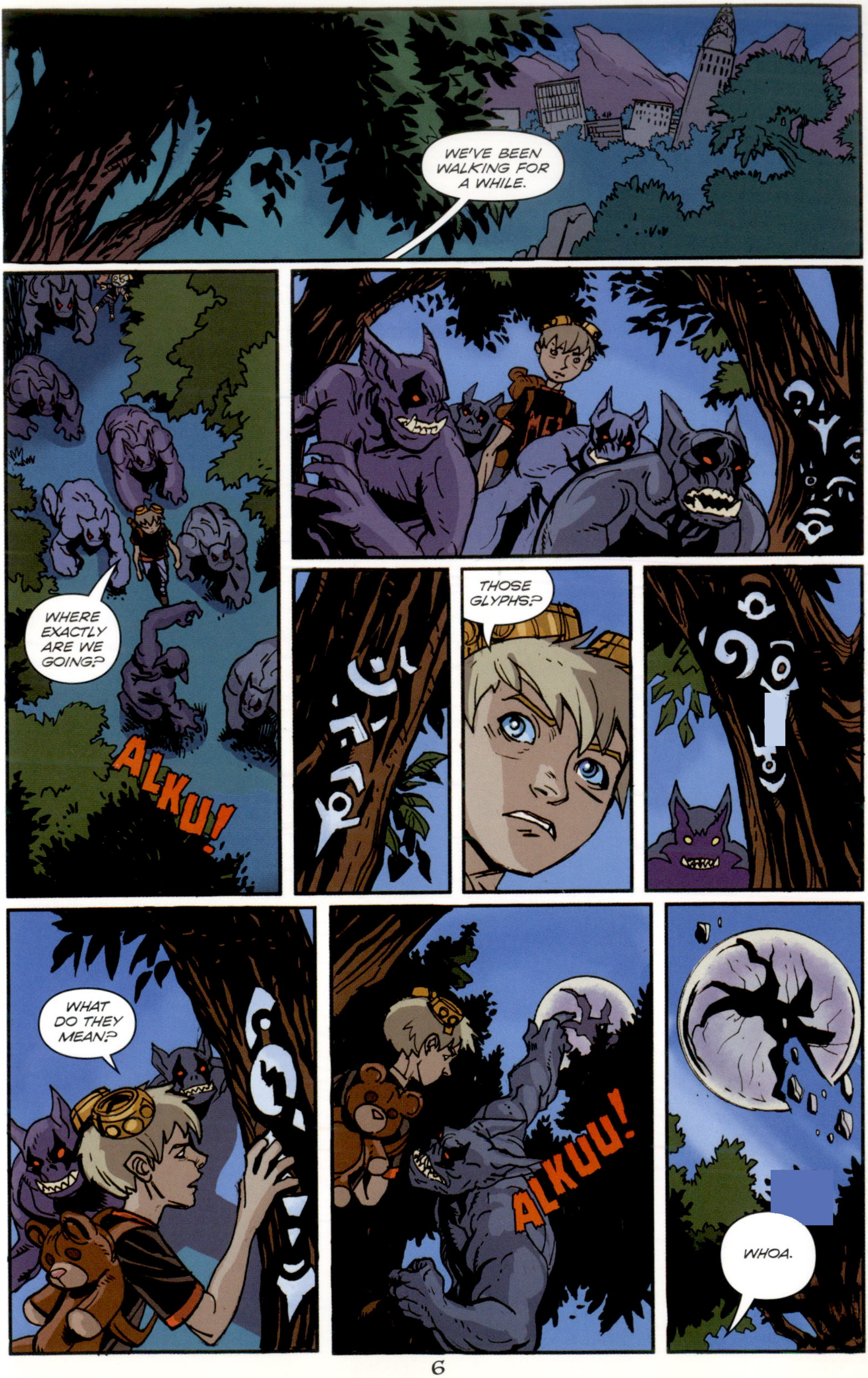
WE'VE BEEN WALKING FOR A WHILE.
WHERE EXACTLY ARE WE GOING?
ALKU!
THOSE GLYPHS?
WHAT DO THEY MEAN?
ALKUU!
WHOA.

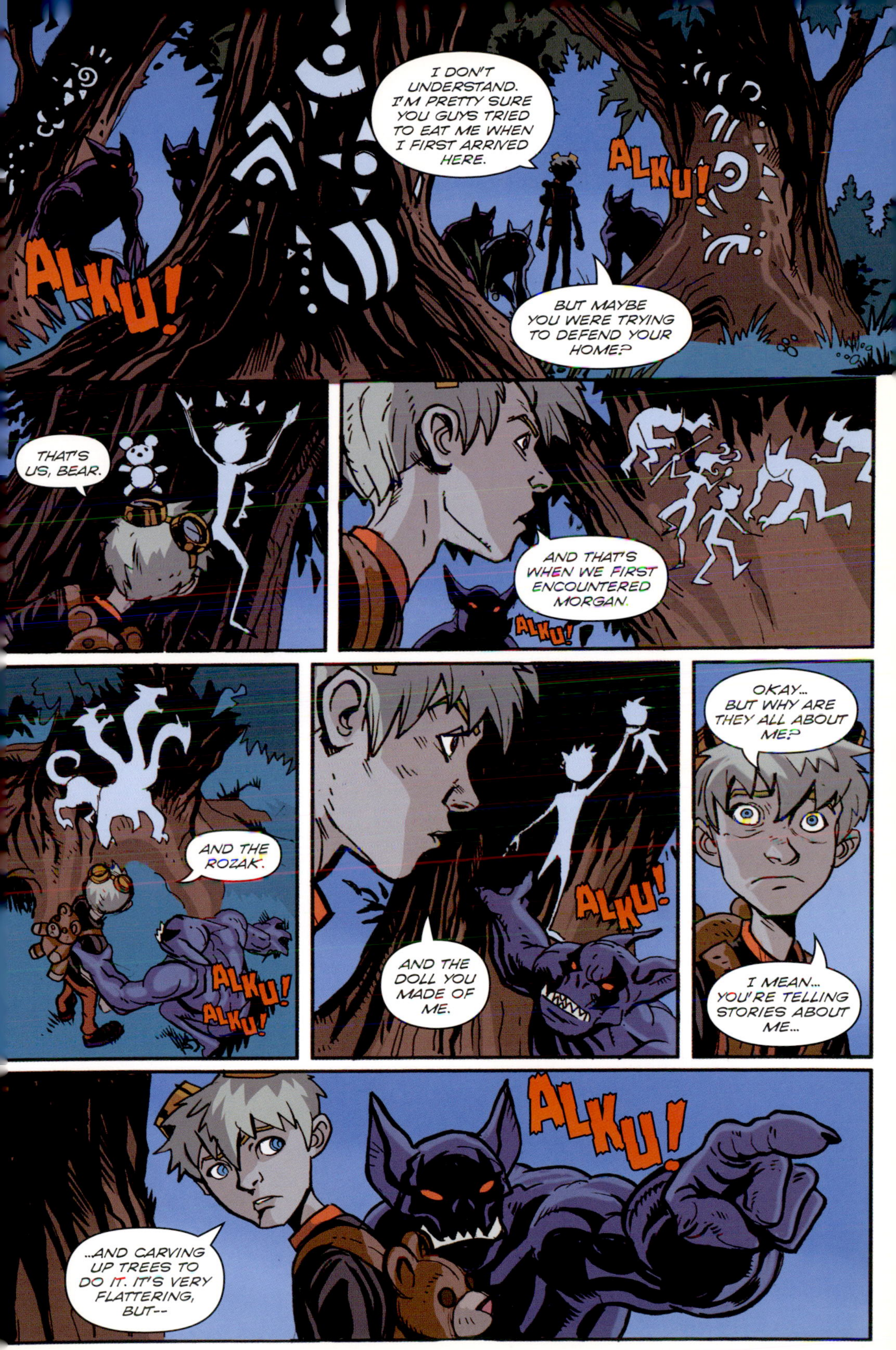
ALKU!
I DON'T UNDERSTAND. I'M PRETTY SURE YOU GUYS TRIED TO EAT ME WHEN I FIRST ARRIVED HERE.
ALKU!
BUT MAYBE YOU WERE TRYING TO DEFEND YOUR HOME?
THAT'S US, BEAR.
AND THAT'S WHEN WE FIRST ENCOUNTERED MORGAN.
ALKU!
AND THE ROZAK.
ALKU!
ALKU!
AND THE DOLL YOU MADE OF ME.
ALKU!
OKAY... BUT WHY ARE THEY ALL ABOUT ME?
I MEAN... YOU'RE TELLING STORIES ABOUT ME...
ALKU!
...AND CARVING UP TREES TO DO IT. IT'S VERY FLATTERING, BUT--

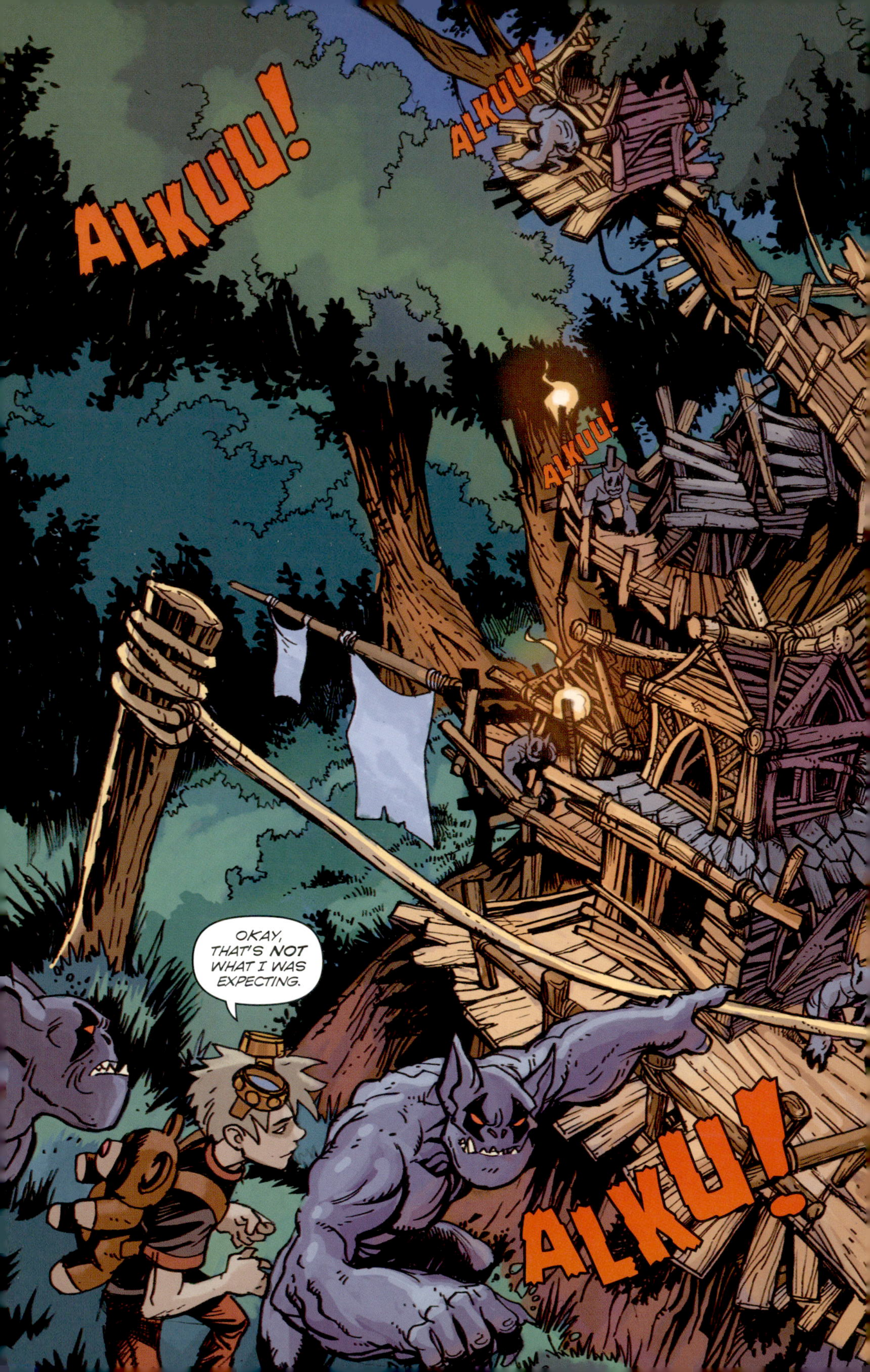
ALKUU!
ALKUU!
ALKUU!
OKAY, THAT'S NOT WHAT I WAS EXPECTING.
ALKU!

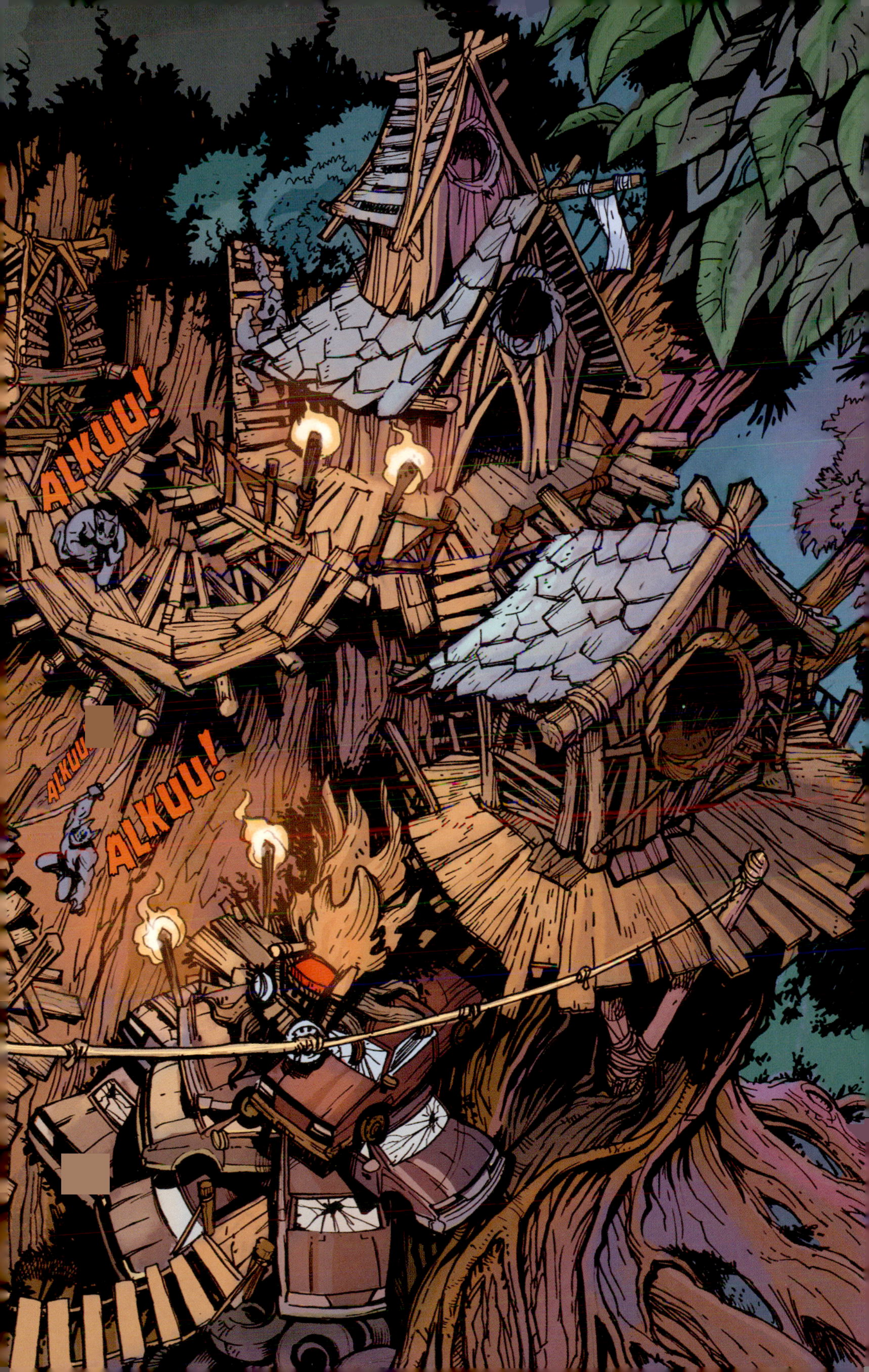
ALKUU!
ALKUU
ALKUU!

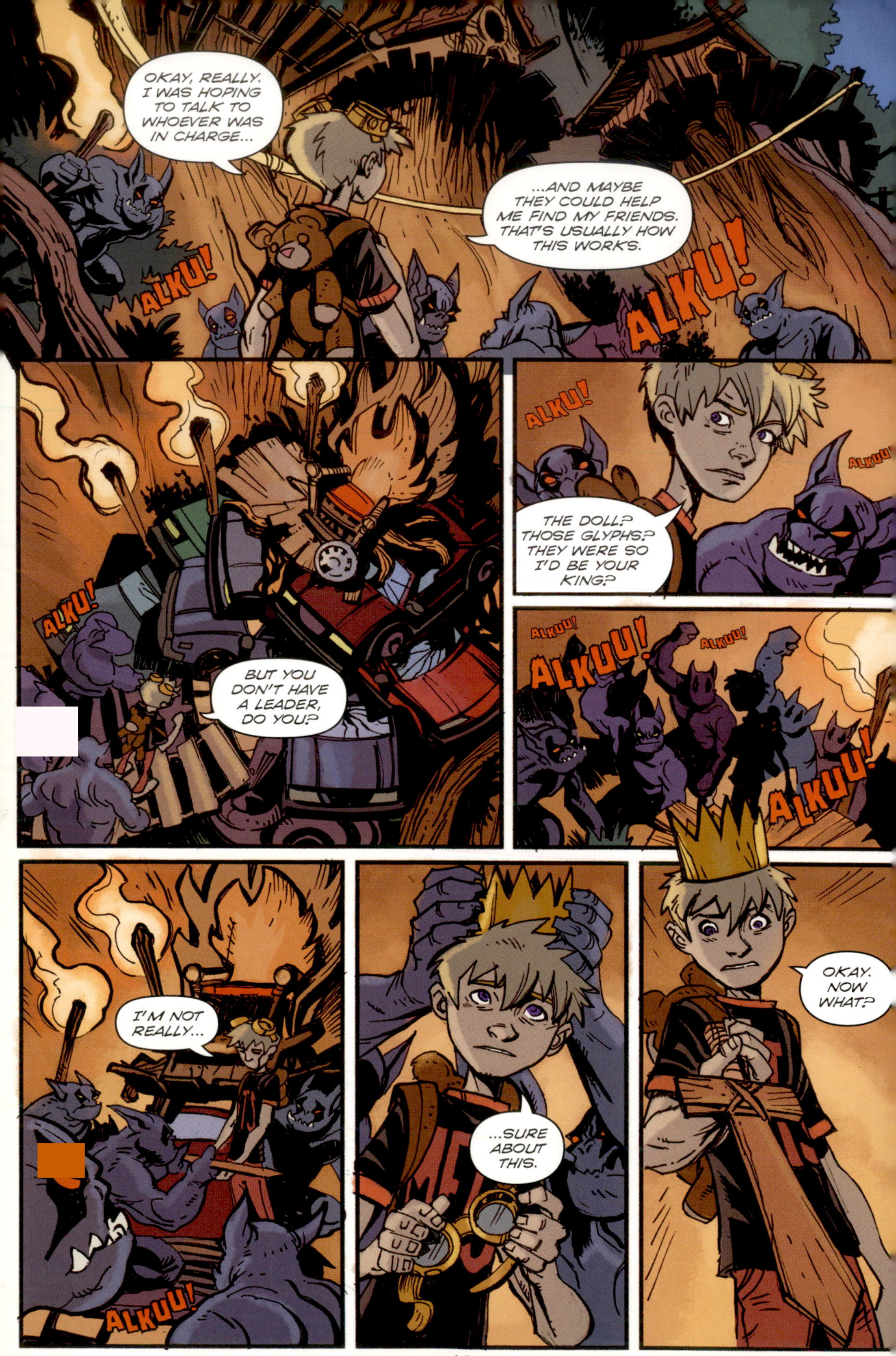
OKAY, REALLY. I WAS HOPING TO TALK TO WHOEVER WAS IN CHARGE...
ALKU!
...AND MAYBE THEY COULD HELP ME FIND MY FRIENDS. THAT'S USUALLY HOW THIS WORKS.
ALKU!
ALKU!
BUT YOU DON'T HAVE A LEADER, DO YOU?
ALKU!
ALKUU
THE DOLL? THOSE GLYPHS? THEY WERE SO I'D BE YOUR KING?
ALKUU!
ALKUU!
ALKUU!
ALKUU!
I'M NOT REALLY...
ALKUU!
...SURE ABOUT THIS.
OKAY. NOW WHAT?

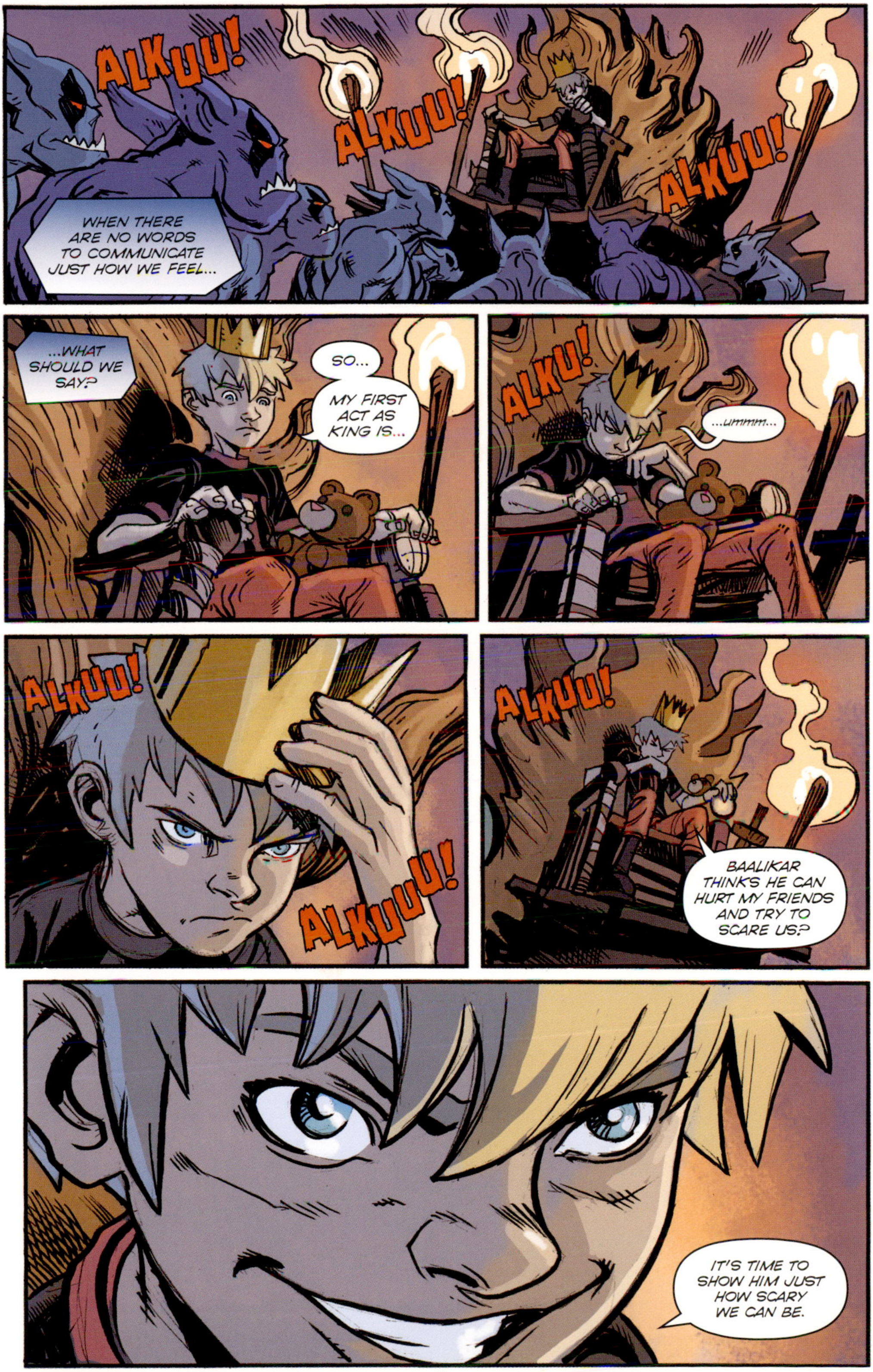
ALKUU!
ALKUU!
ALKUU!
WHEN THERE ARE NO WORDS TO COMMUNICATE JUST HOW WE FEEL...
...WHAT SHOULD WE SAY?
SO...
MY FIRST ACT AS KING IS...
ALKU!
...ummm...
ALKUU!
ALKUUU!
ALKUU!
BAALIKAR THINKS HE CAN HURT MY FRIENDS AND TRY TO SCARE US?
IT'S TIME TO SHOW HIM JUST HOW SCARY WE CAN BE.

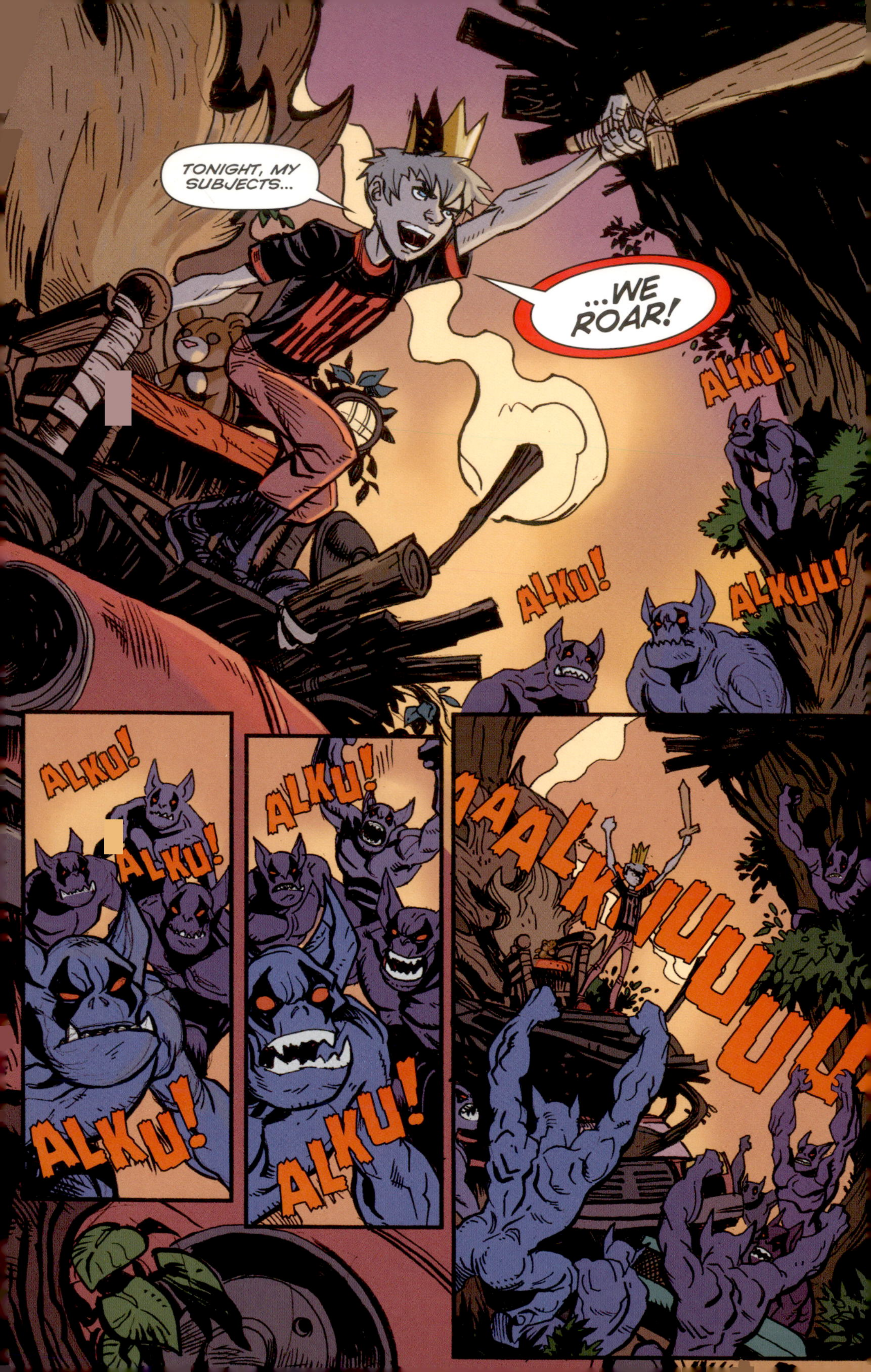
TONIGHT, MY SUBJECTS...
...WE ROAR!
ALKU!
ALKU!
ALKUU!
ALKU!
ALKU!
ALKU!
ALKU!
ALKU!
AAALKUUUUU

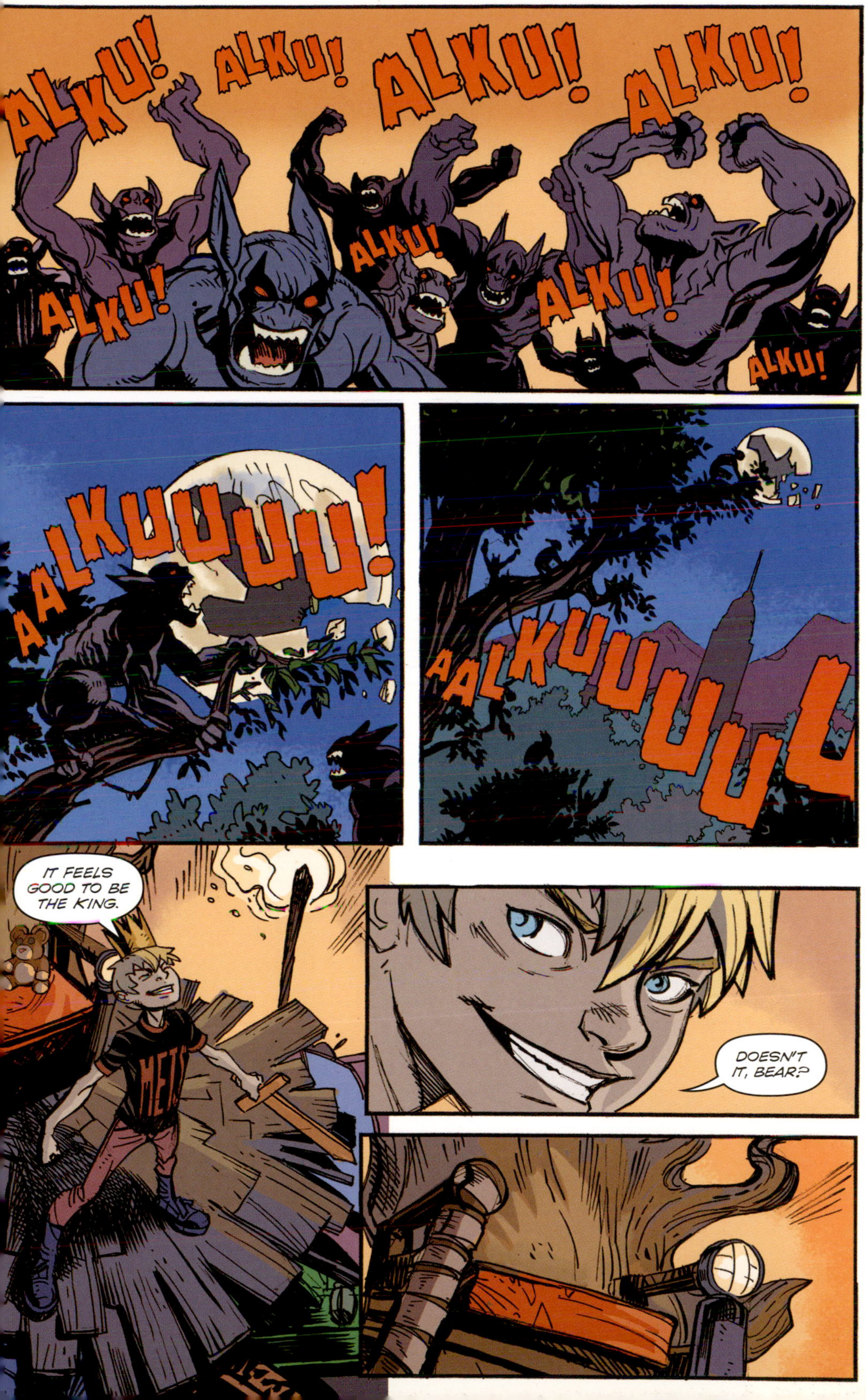
ALKU!
ALKU!
ALKU!
ALKU!
ALKU!
ALKU!
ALKU!
ALKU!
AALKUUUUU!
AALKUUUUUU
IT FEELS GOOD TO BE THE KING.
DOESN'T IT, BEAR?

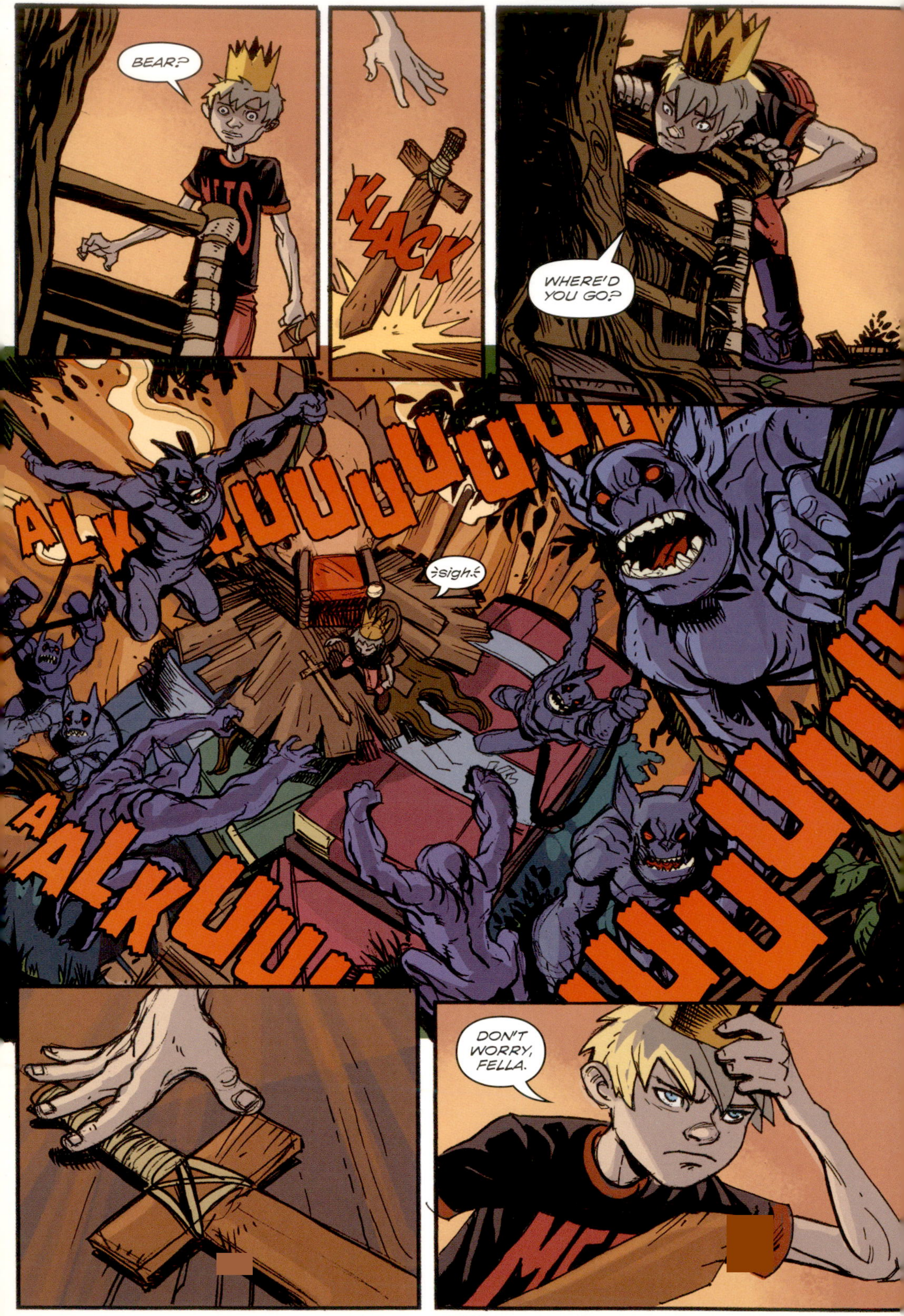
BEAR?
KLACK
WHERE'D YOU GO?
ALKUUUUUUUUUU
sigh.
AALKUUUUUUUUUU
DON'T WORRY, FELLA.

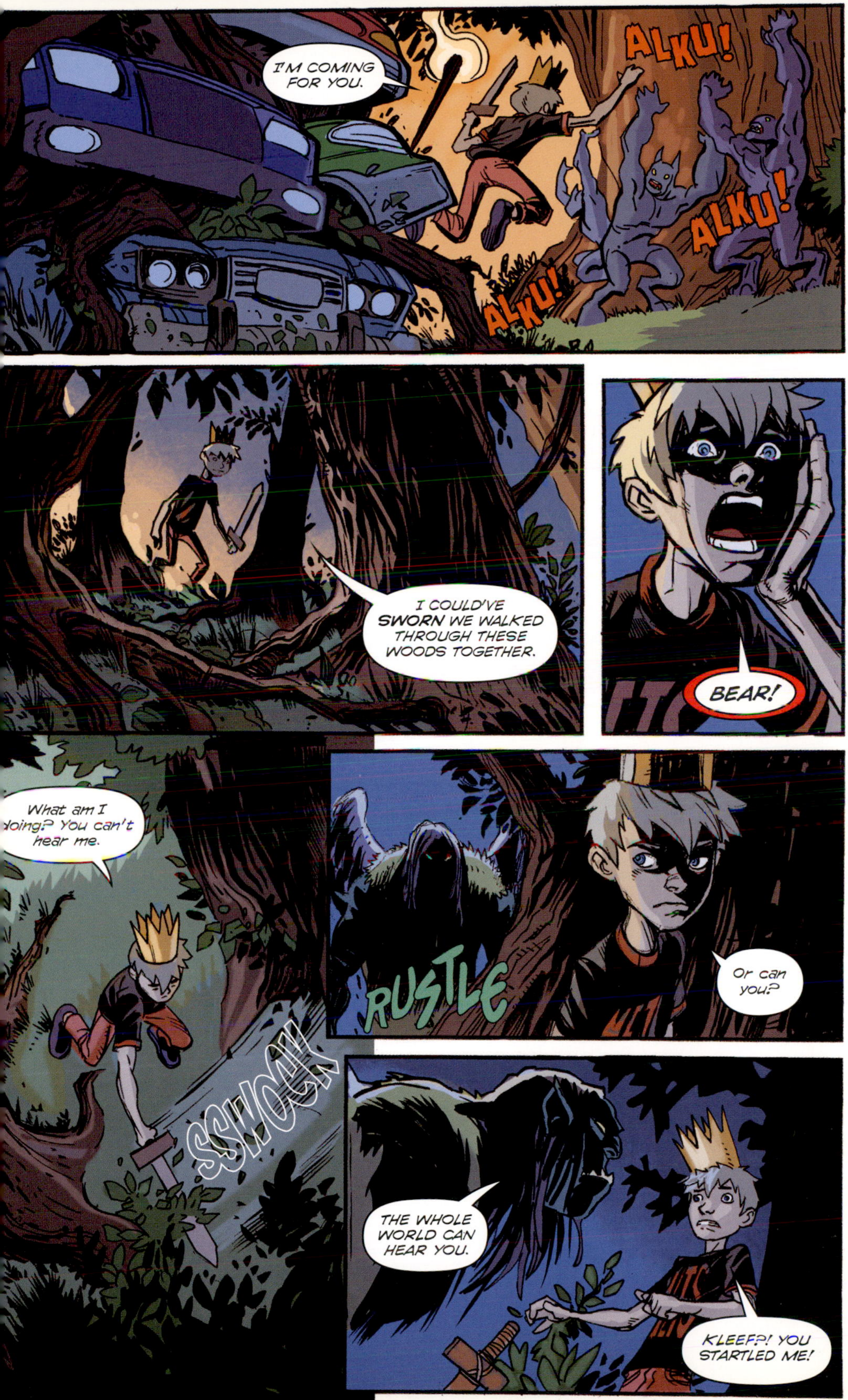
I'M COMING FOR YOU.
ALKU!
ALKU!
ALKU!
I COULD'VE **SWORN** WE WALKED THROUGH THESE WOODS TOGETHER.
BEAR!
What am I doing? You can't hear me.
SSWOCK
RUSTLE
Or can you?
THE WHOLE WORLD CAN HEAR YOU.
KLEEF?! YOU STARTLED ME!

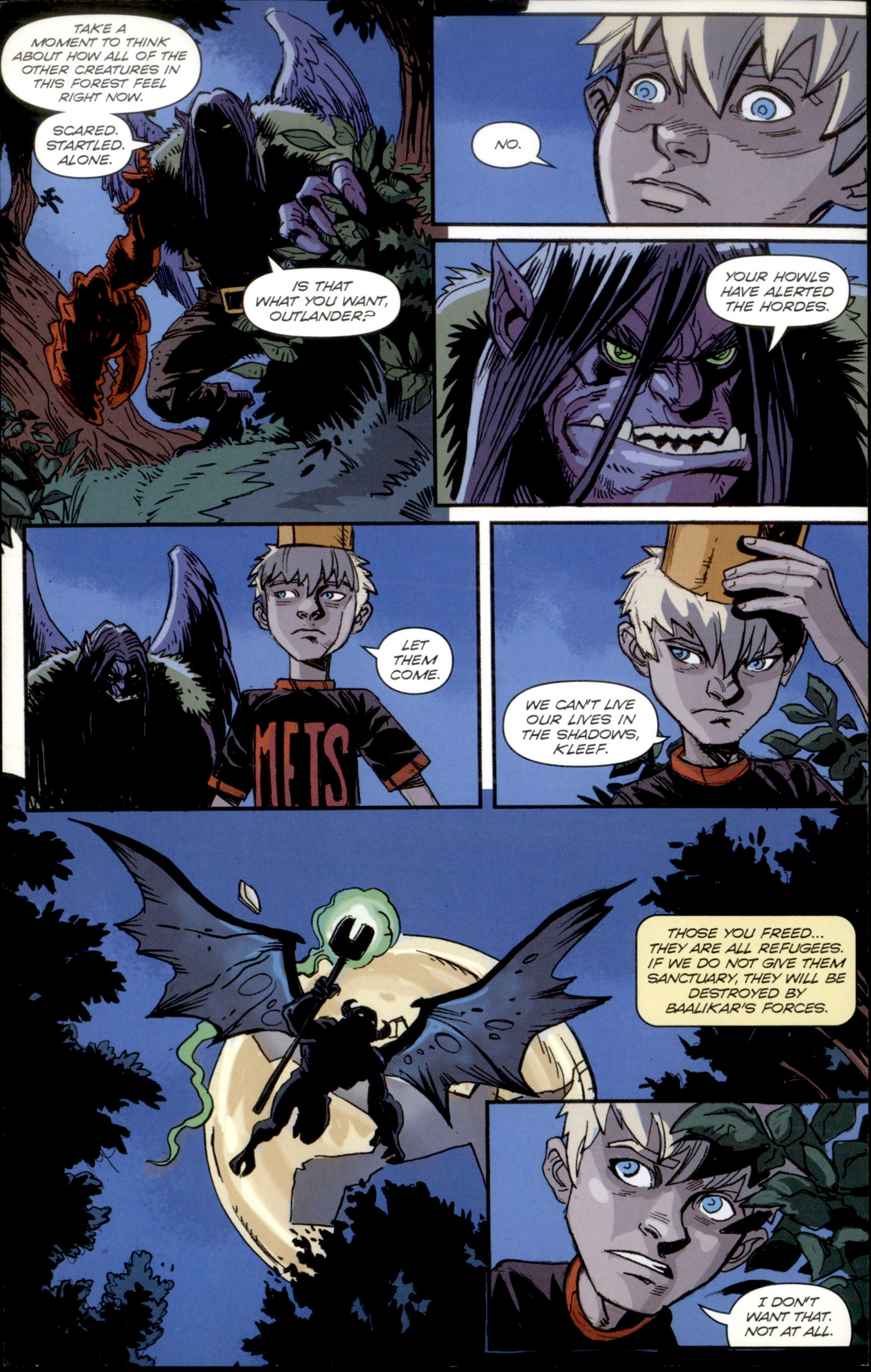
TAKE A MOMENT TO THINK ABOUT HOW ALL OF THE OTHER CREATURES IN THIS FOREST FEEL RIGHT NOW.
SCARED. STARTLED. ALONE.
IS THAT WHAT YOU WANT, OUTLANDER?
NO.
YOUR HOWLS HAVE ALERTED THE HORDES.
LET THEM COME.
METS
WE CAN'T LIVE OUR LIVES IN THE SHADOWS, KLEEF.
THOSE YOU FREED... THEY ARE ALL REFUGEES. IF WE DO NOT GIVE THEM SANCTUARY, THEY WILL BE DESTROYED BY BAALIKAR'S FORCES.
I DON'T WANT THAT. NOT AT ALL.

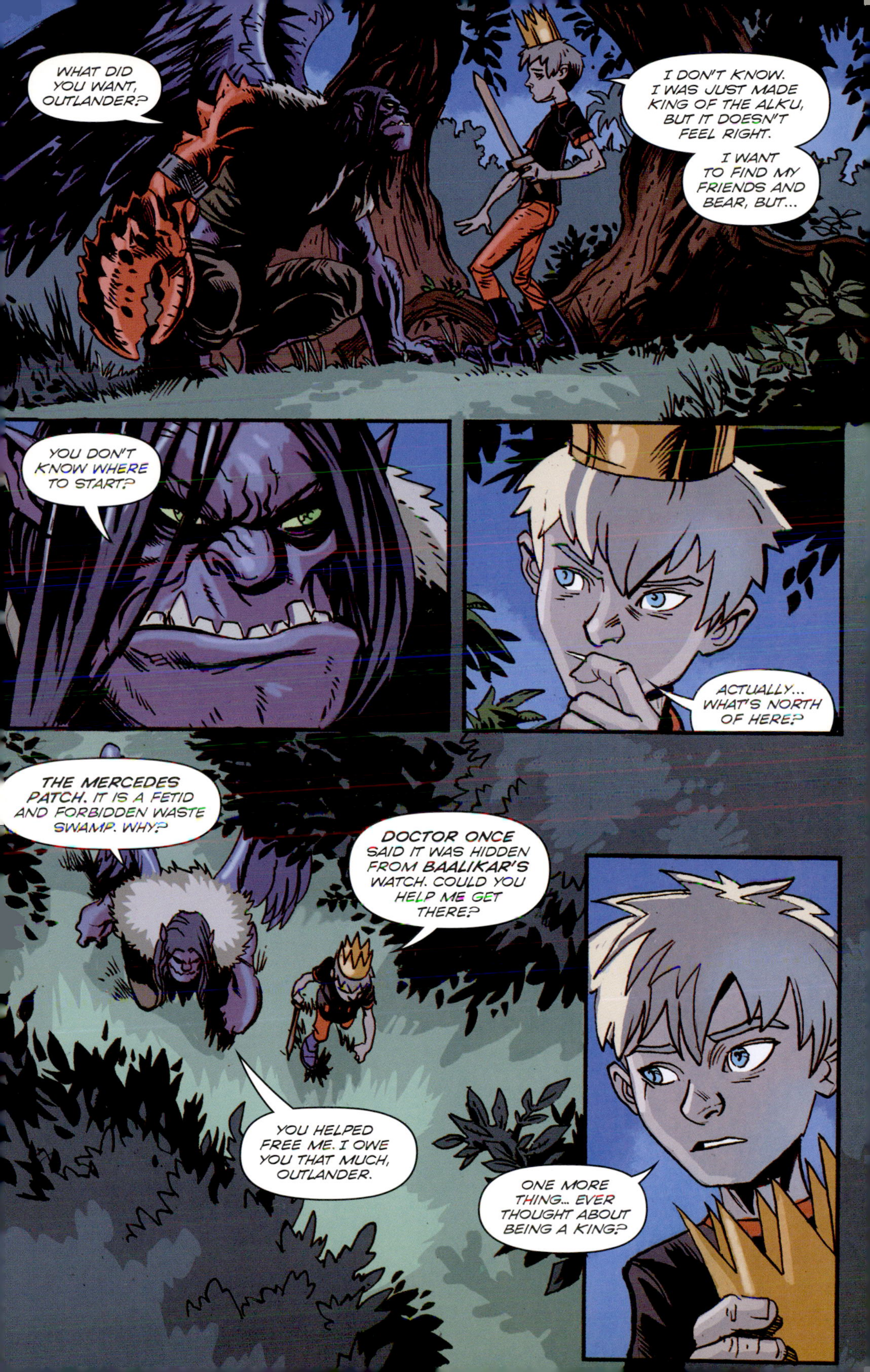
WHAT DID YOU WANT, OUTLANDER?
I DON'T KNOW. I WAS JUST MADE KING OF THE ALKU, BUT IT DOESN'T FEEL RIGHT.
I WANT TO FIND MY FRIENDS AND BEAR, BUT...
YOU DON'T KNOW WHERE TO START?
ACTUALLY... WHAT'S NORTH OF HERE?
THE MERCEDES PATCH. IT IS A FETID AND FORBIDDEN WASTE SWAMP. WHY?
DOCTOR ONCE SAID IT WAS HIDDEN FROM BAALIKAR'S WATCH. COULD YOU HELP ME GET THERE?
YOU HELPED FREE ME. I OWE YOU THAT MUCH, OUTLANDER.
ONE MORE THING... EVER THOUGHT ABOUT BEING A KING?

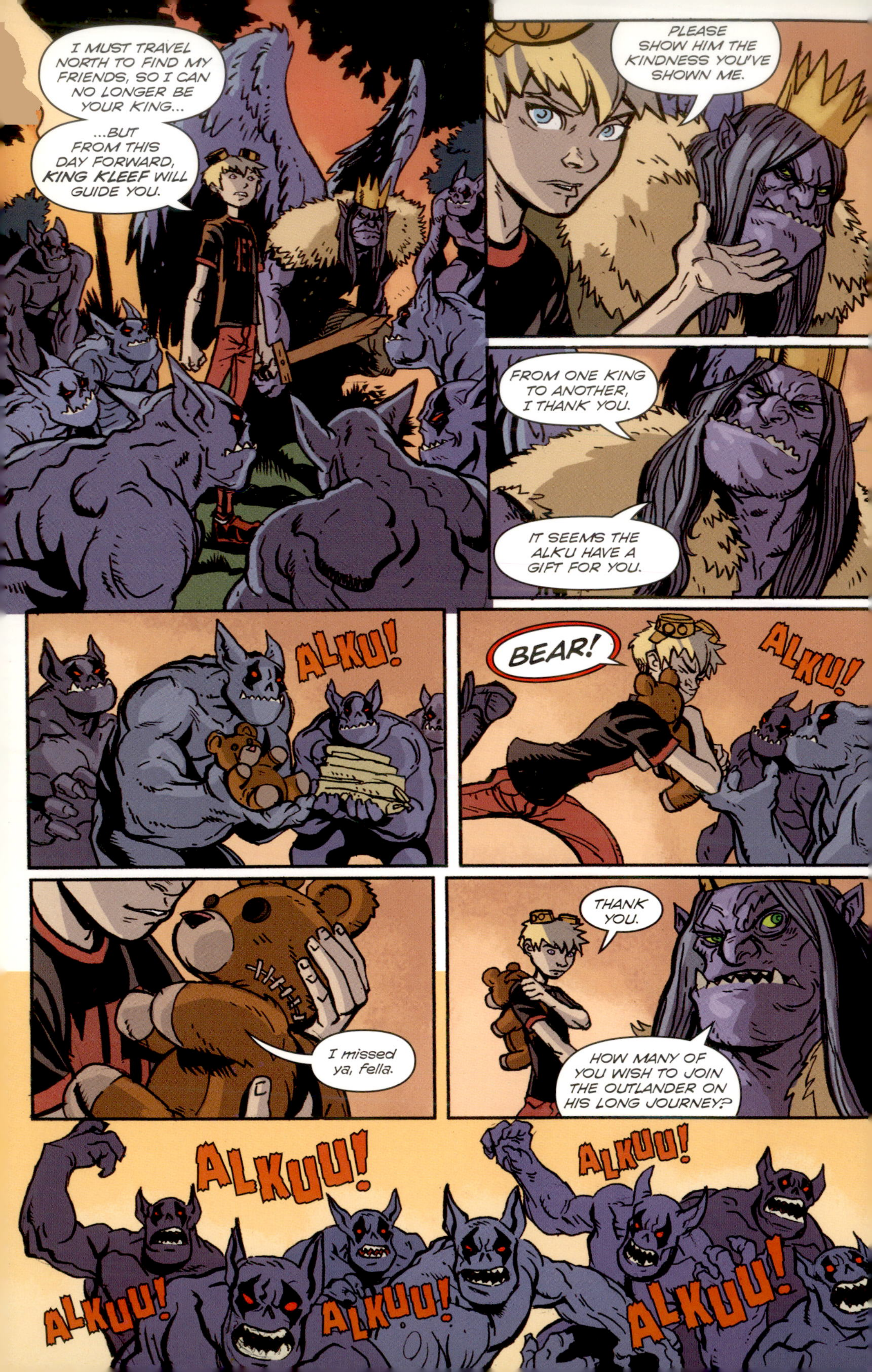
I MUST TRAVEL NORTH TO FIND MY FRIENDS, SO I CAN NO LONGER BE YOUR KING...
...BUT FROM THIS DAY FORWARD, KING KLEEF WILL GUIDE YOU.
PLEASE SHOW HIM THE KINDNESS YOU'VE SHOWN ME.
FROM ONE KING TO ANOTHER, I THANK YOU.
IT SEEMS THE ALKU HAVE A GIFT FOR YOU.
ALKU!
BEAR!
ALKU!
I missed ya, fella.
THANK YOU.
HOW MANY OF YOU WISH TO JOIN THE OUTLANDER ON HIS LONG JOURNEY?
ALKUU!
ALKUU!
ALKUU!
ALKUU!
ALKUU!

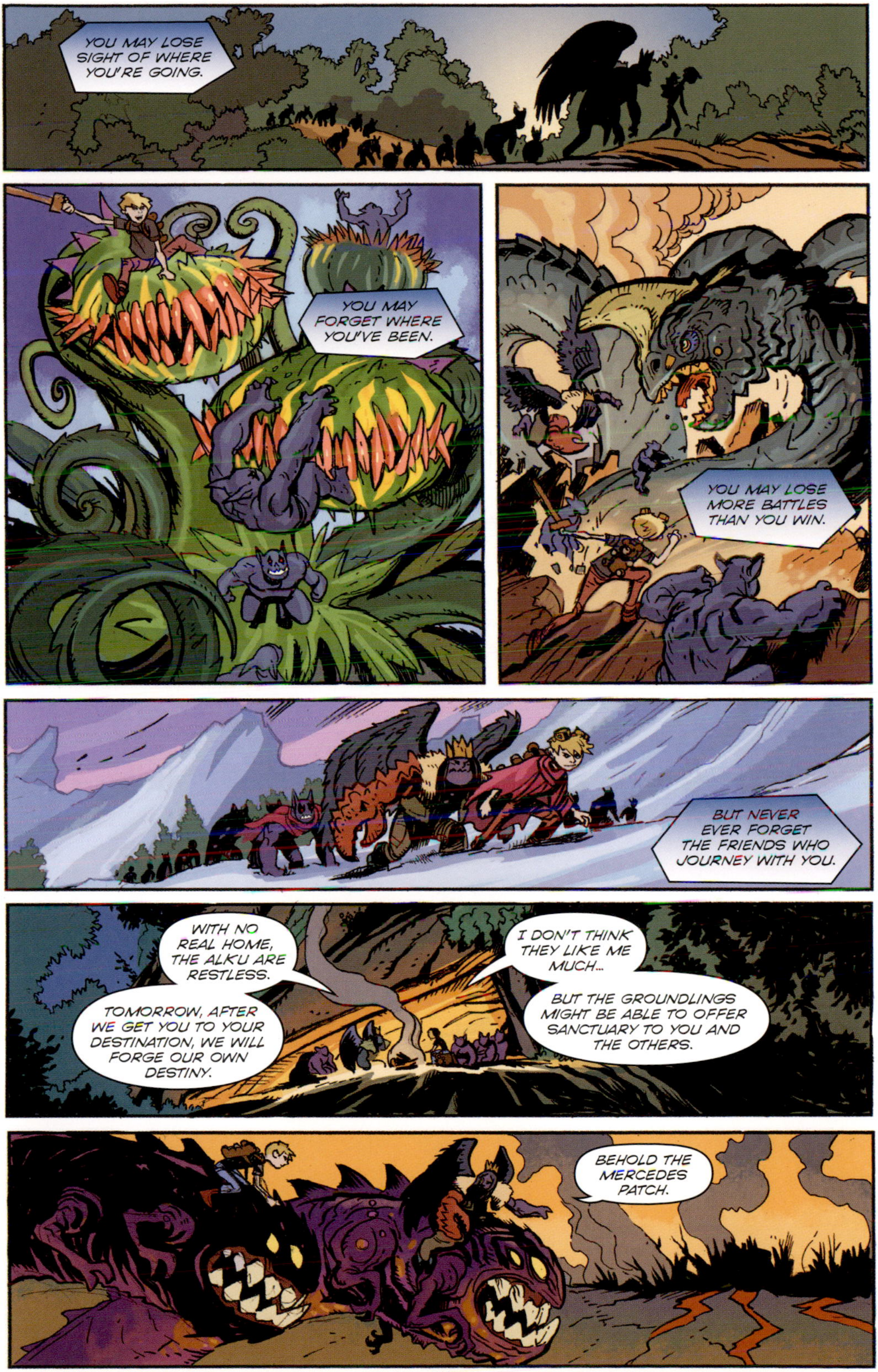
YOU MAY LOSE SIGHT OF WHERE YOU'RE GOING.
YOU MAY FORGET WHERE YOU'VE BEEN.
YOU MAY LOSE MORE BATTLES THAN YOU WIN.
BUT NEVER EVER FORGET THE FRIENDS WHO JOURNEY WITH YOU.
WITH NO REAL HOME, THE ALKU ARE RESTLESS.
TOMORROW, AFTER WE GET YOU TO YOUR DESTINATION, WE WILL FORGE OUR OWN DESTINY.
I DON'T THINK THEY LIKE ME MUCH...
BUT THE GROUNDLINGS MIGHT BE ABLE TO OFFER SANCTUARY TO YOU AND THE OTHERS.
BEHOLD THE MERCEDES PATCH.

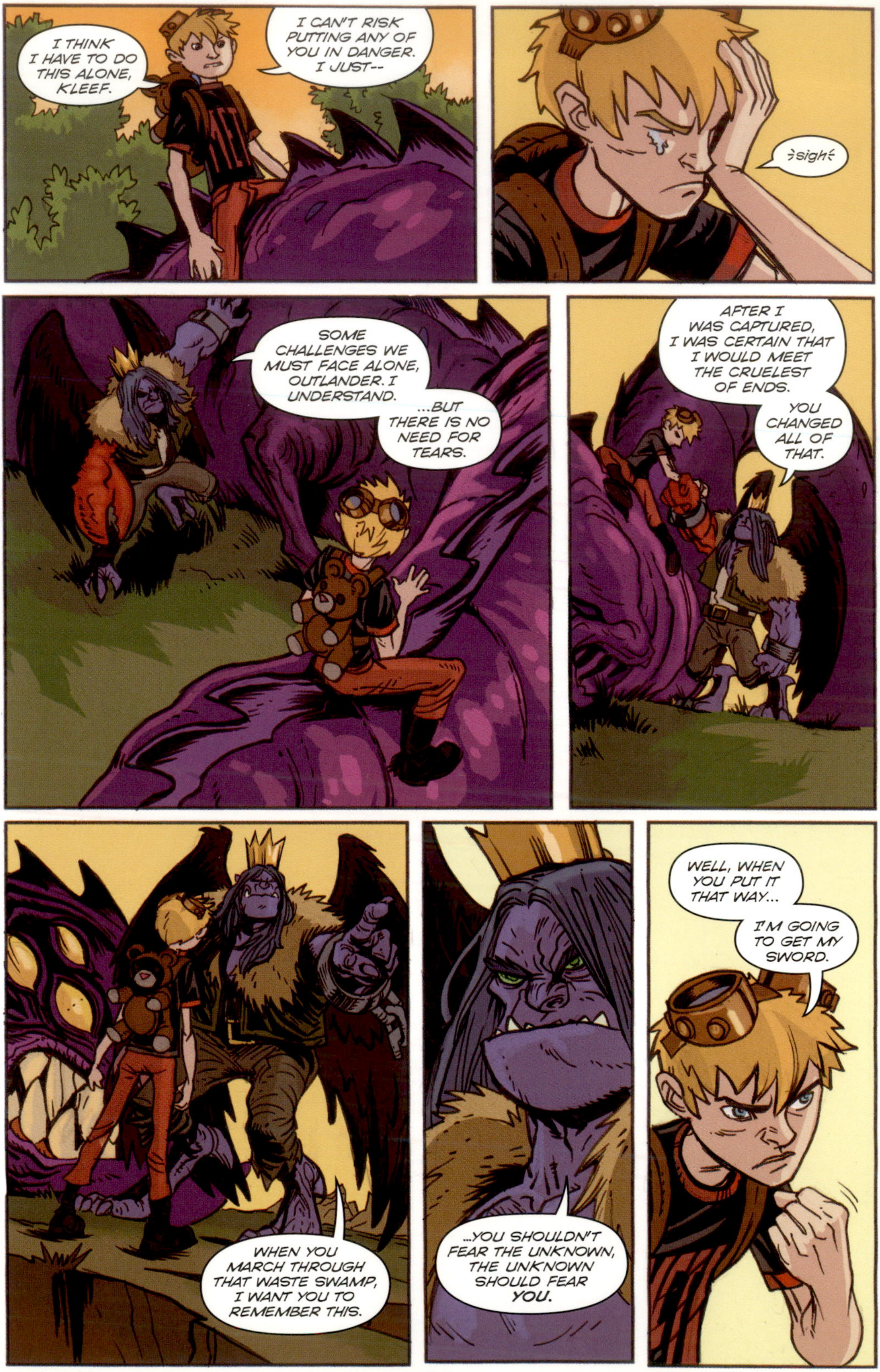
I THINK I HAVE TO DO THIS ALONE, KLEEF.
I CAN'T RISK PUTTING ANY OF YOU IN DANGER. I JUST--
sigh
SOME CHALLENGES WE MUST FACE ALONE, OUTLANDER. I UNDERSTAND.
...BUT THERE IS NO NEED FOR TEARS.
AFTER I WAS CAPTURED, I WAS CERTAIN THAT I WOULD MEET THE CRUELEST OF ENDS.
YOU CHANGED ALL OF THAT.
WHEN YOU MARCH THROUGH THAT WASTE SWAMP, I WANT YOU TO REMEMBER THIS.
...YOU SHOULDN'T FEAR THE UNKNOWN, THE UNKNOWN SHOULD FEAR YOU.
WELL, WHEN YOU PUT IT THAT WAY...
I'M GOING TO GET MY SWORD.

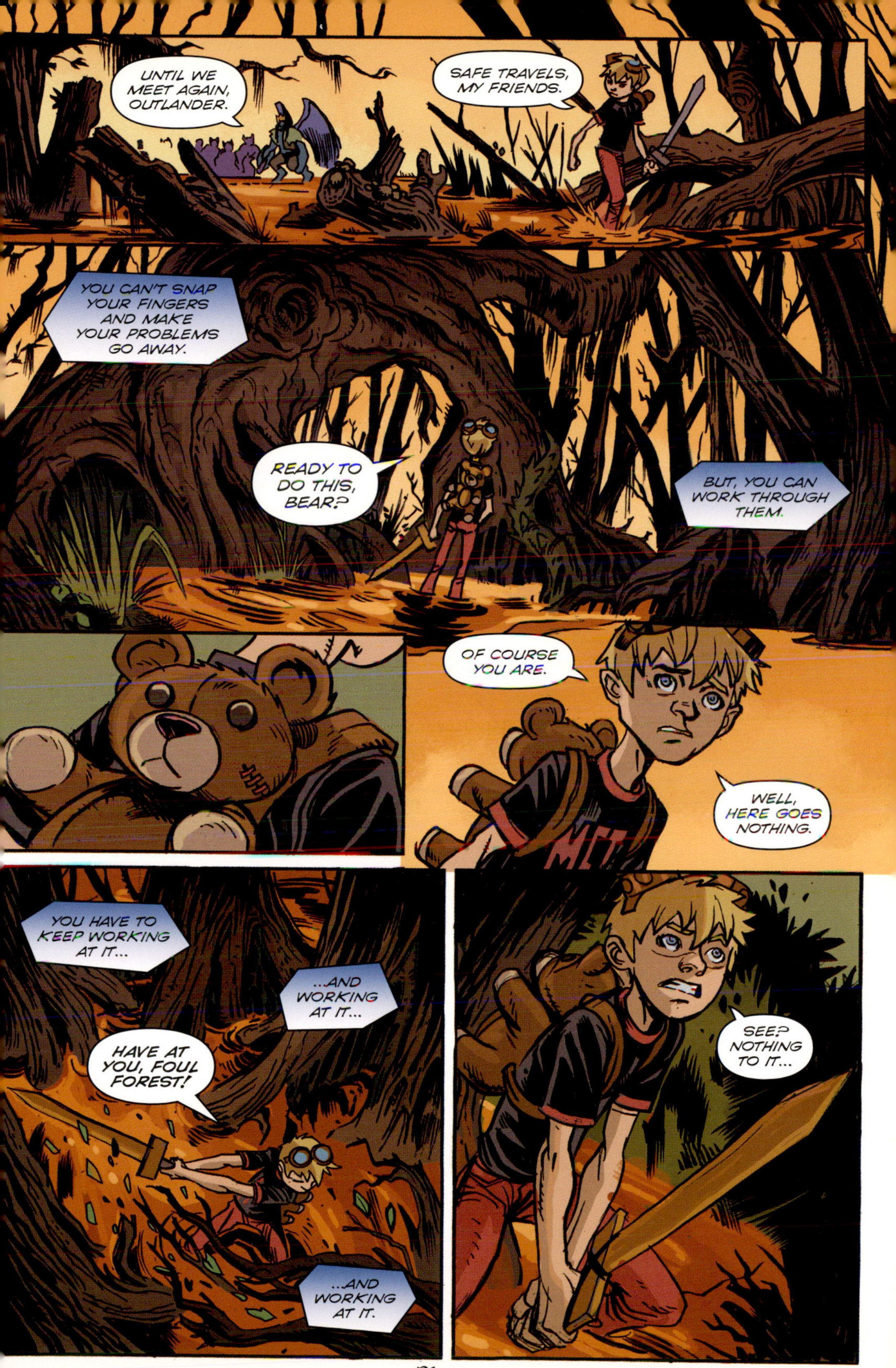
UNTIL WE MEET AGAIN, OUTLANDER.
SAFE TRAVELS, MY FRIENDS.
YOU CAN'T SNAP YOUR FINGERS AND MAKE YOUR PROBLEMS GO AWAY.
READY TO DO THIS, BEAR?
BUT, YOU CAN WORK THROUGH THEM.
OF COURSE YOU ARE.
WELL, HERE GOES NOTHING.
YOU HAVE TO KEEP WORKING AT IT...
...AND WORKING AT IT...
HAVE AT YOU, FOUL FOREST!
...AND WORKING AT IT.
SEE? NOTHING TO IT...

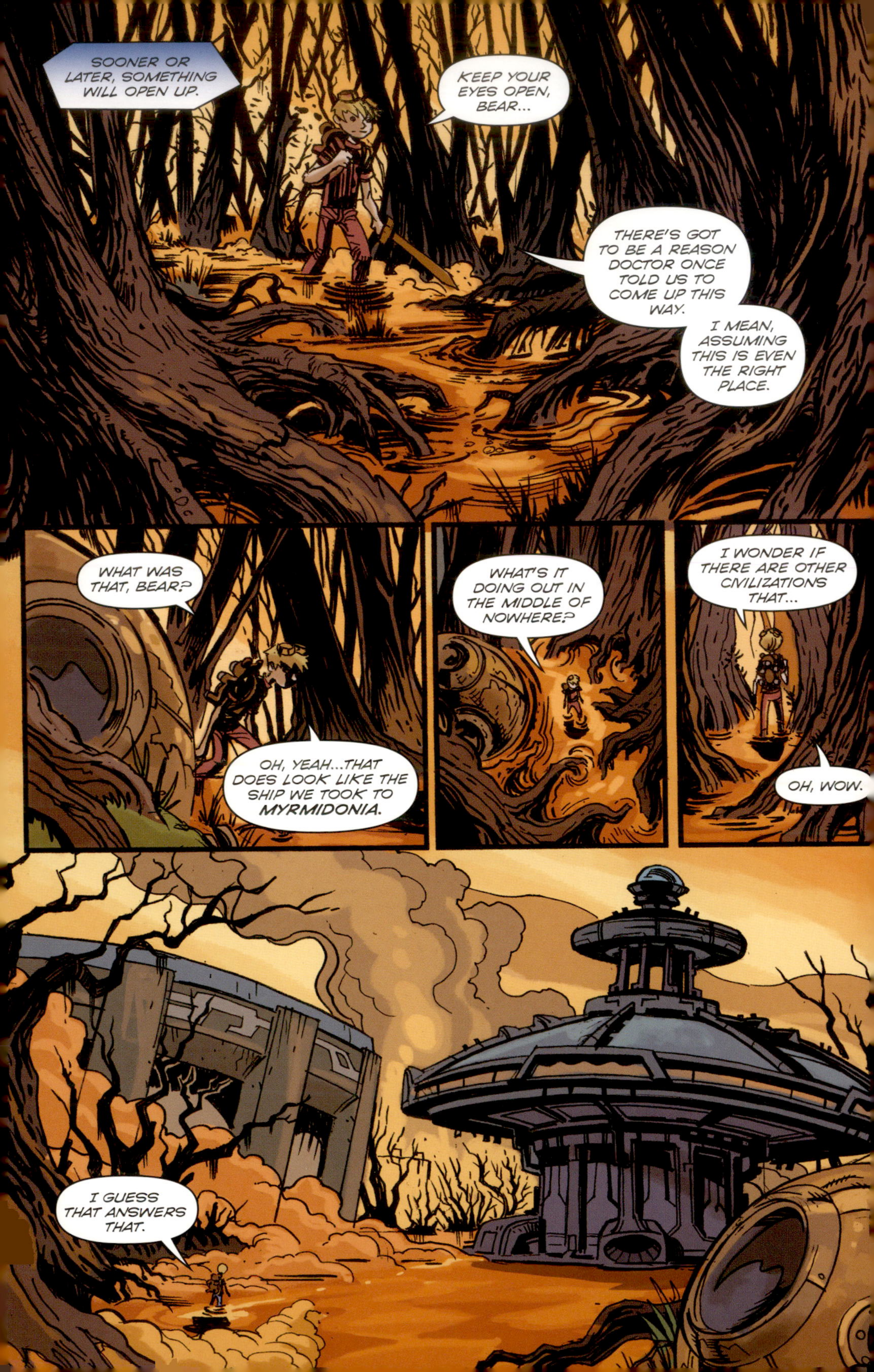
SOONER OR LATER, SOMETHING WILL OPEN UP.
KEEP YOUR EYES OPEN, BEAR...
THERE'S GOT TO BE A REASON DOCTOR ONCE TOLD US TO COME UP THIS WAY.
I MEAN, ASSUMING THIS IS EVEN THE RIGHT PLACE.
WHAT WAS THAT, BEAR?
OH, YEAH...THAT DOES LOOK LIKE THE SHIP WE TOOK TO **MYRMIDONIA**.
WHAT'S IT DOING OUT IN THE MIDDLE OF NOWHERE?
I WONDER IF THERE ARE OTHER CIVILIZATIONS THAT...
OH, WOW.
I GUESS THAT ANSWERS THAT.

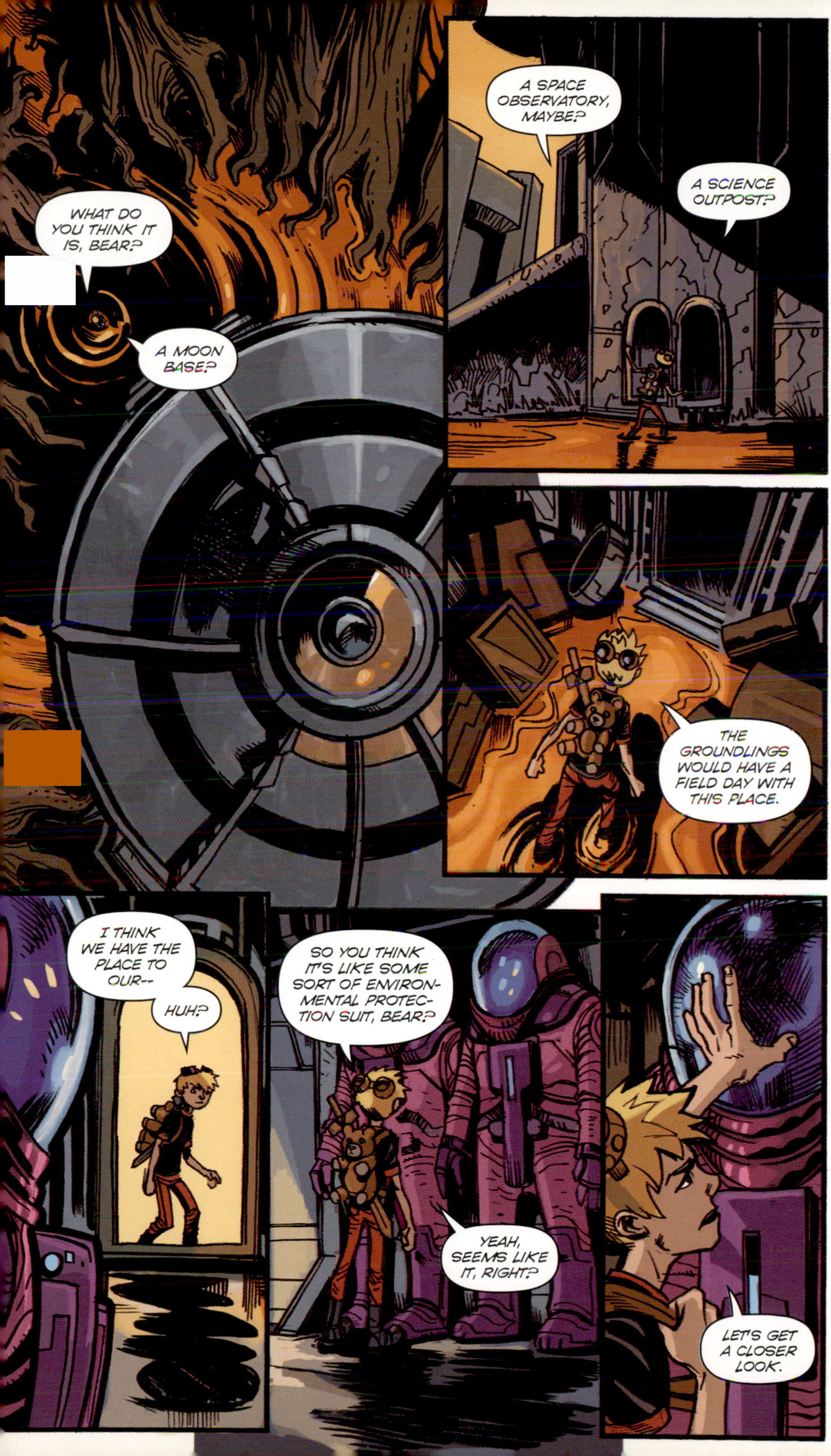
WHAT DO YOU THINK IT IS, BEAR?
A MOON BASE?
A SPACE OBSERVATORY, MAYBE?
A SCIENCE OUTPOST?
THE GROUNDLINGS WOULD HAVE A FIELD DAY WITH THIS PLACE.
I THINK WE HAVE THE PLACE TO OUR--
HUH?
SO YOU THINK IT'S LIKE SOME SORT OF ENVIRONMENTAL PROTECTION SUIT, BEAR?
YEAH, SEEMS LIKE IT, RIGHT?
LET'S GET A CLOSER LOOK.

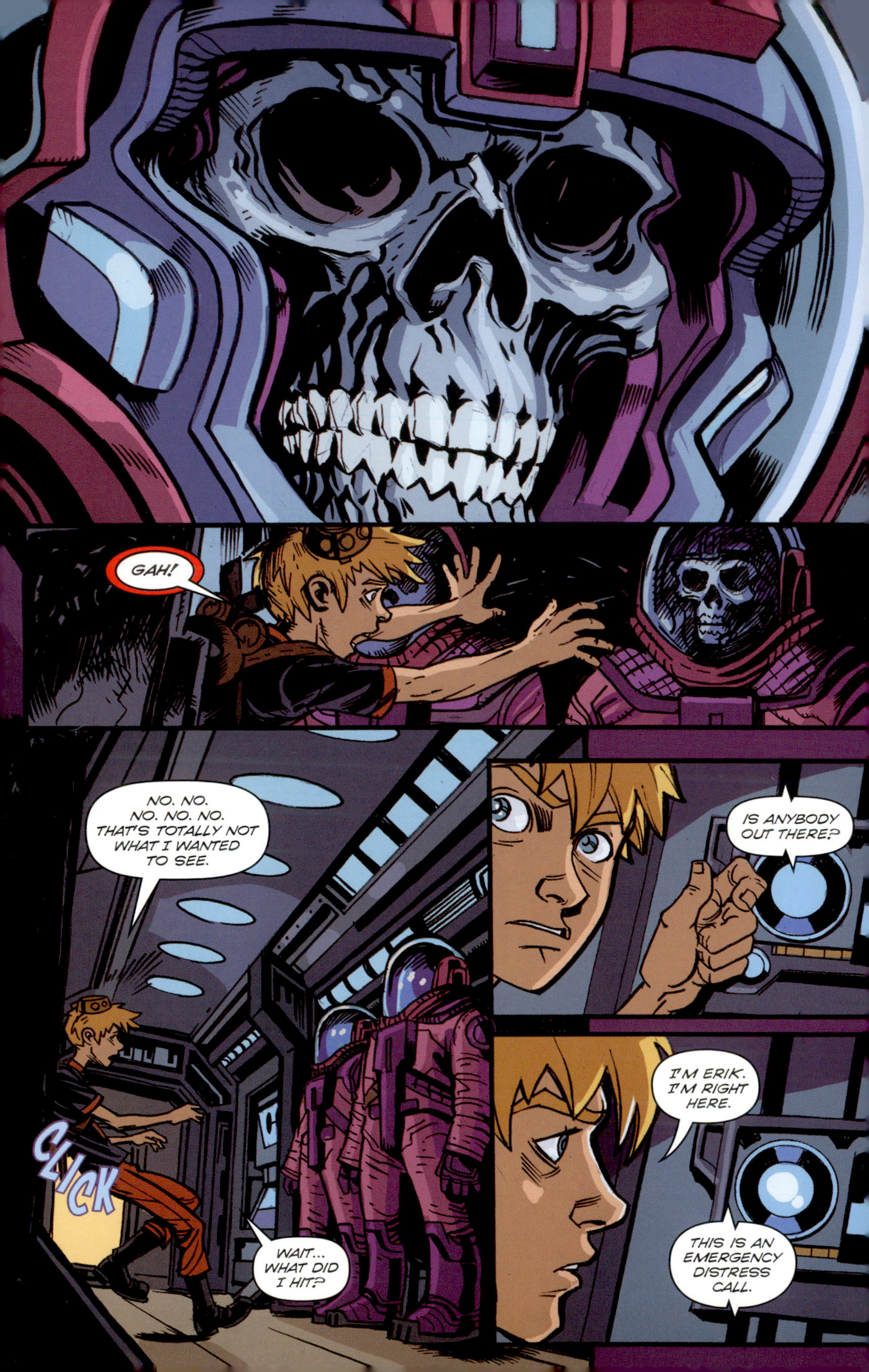
GAH!
NO. NO. NO. NO. NO. THAT'S TOTALLY NOT WHAT I WANTED TO SEE.
CLICK
WAIT... WHAT DID I HIT?
IS ANYBODY OUT THERE?
I'M ERIK. I'M RIGHT HERE.
THIS IS AN EMERGENCY DISTRESS CALL.

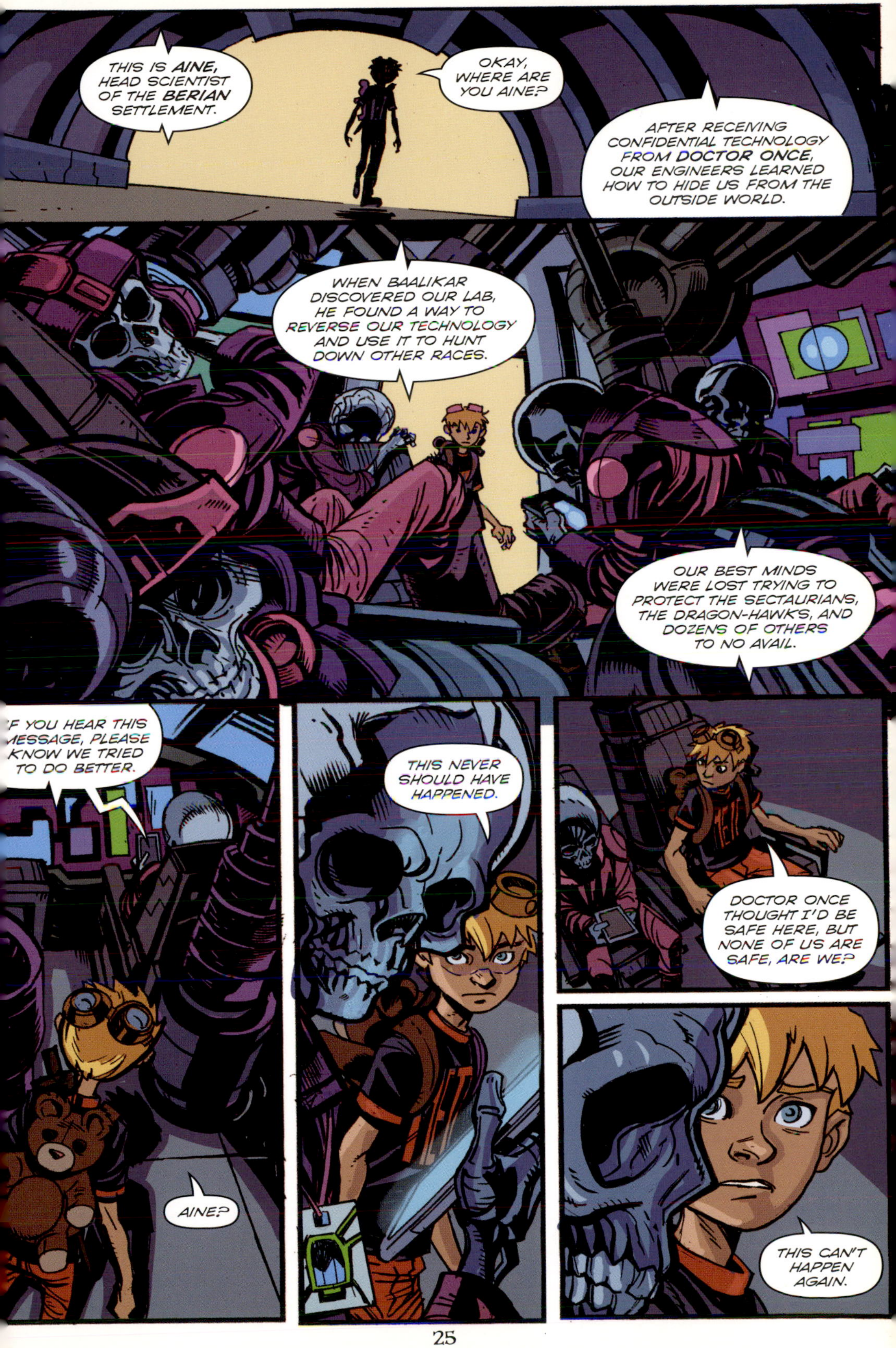

THIS IS AINE, HEAD SCIENTIST OF THE BERIAN SETTLEMENT.
OKAY, WHERE ARE YOU AINE?
AFTER RECEIVING CONFIDENTIAL TECHNOLOGY FROM DOCTOR ONCE, OUR ENGINEERS LEARNED HOW TO HIDE US FROM THE OUTSIDE WORLD.
WHEN BAALIKAR DISCOVERED OUR LAB, HE FOUND A WAY TO REVERSE OUR TECHNOLOGY AND USE IT TO HUNT DOWN OTHER RACES.
OUR BEST MINDS WERE LOST TRYING TO PROTECT THE SECTAURIANS, THE DRAGON-HAWKS, AND DOZENS OF OTHERS TO NO AVAIL.
F YOU HEAR THIS MESSAGE, PLEASE KNOW WE TRIED TO DO BETTER.
AINE?
THIS NEVER SHOULD HAVE HAPPENED.
DOCTOR ONCE THOUGHT I'D BE SAFE HERE, BUT NONE OF US ARE SAFE, ARE WE?
THIS CAN'T HAPPEN AGAIN.

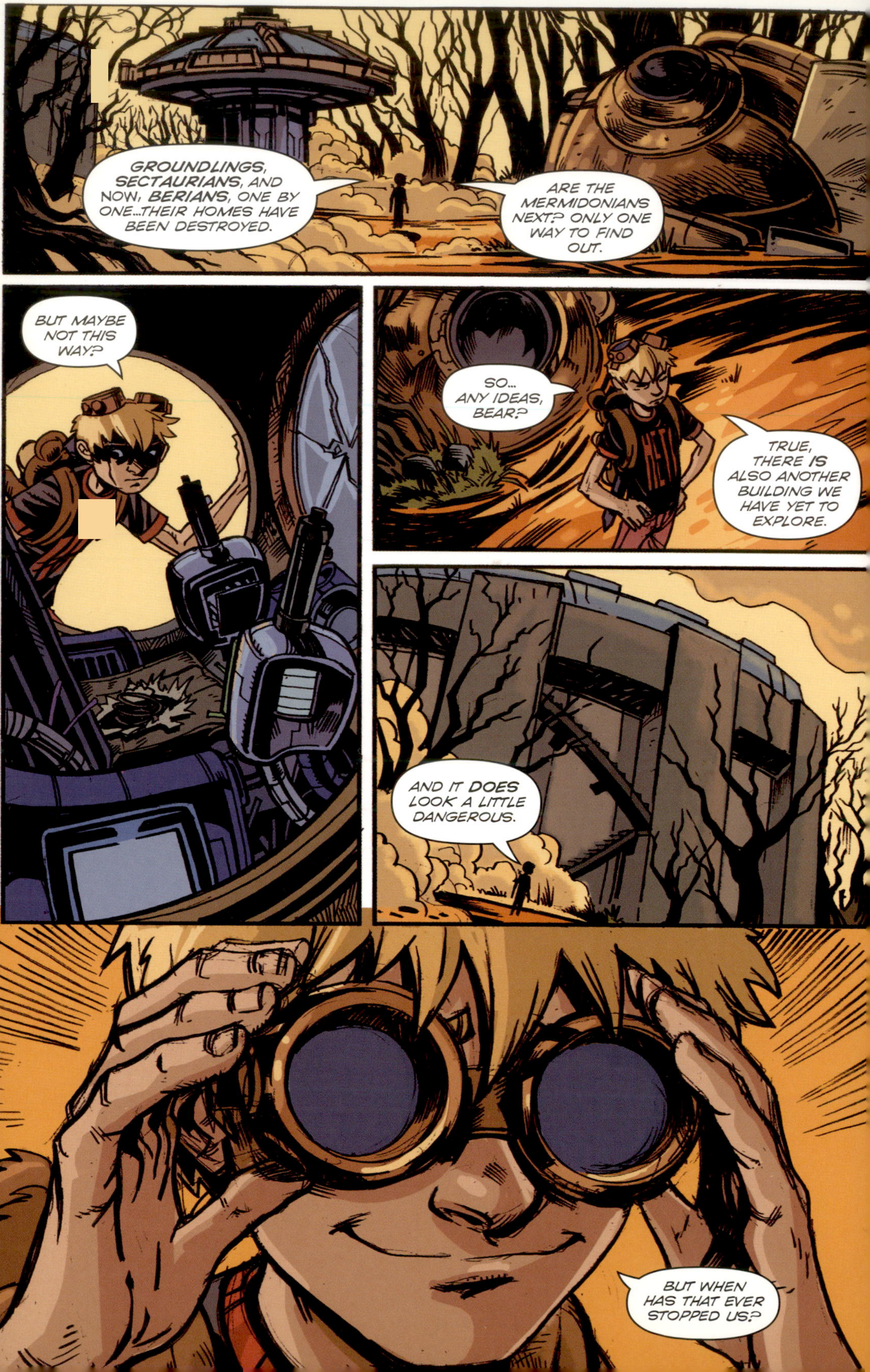
GROUNDLINGS, SECTAURIANS, AND NOW, BERIANS, ONE BY ONE...THEIR HOMES HAVE BEEN DESTROYED.
ARE THE MERMIDONIANS NEXT? ONLY ONE WAY TO FIND OUT.
BUT MAYBE NOT THIS WAY?
SO... ANY IDEAS, BEAR?
TRUE, THERE IS ALSO ANOTHER BUILDING WE HAVE YET TO EXPLORE.
AND IT DOES LOOK A LITTLE DANGEROUS.
BUT WHEN HAS THAT EVER STOPPED US?

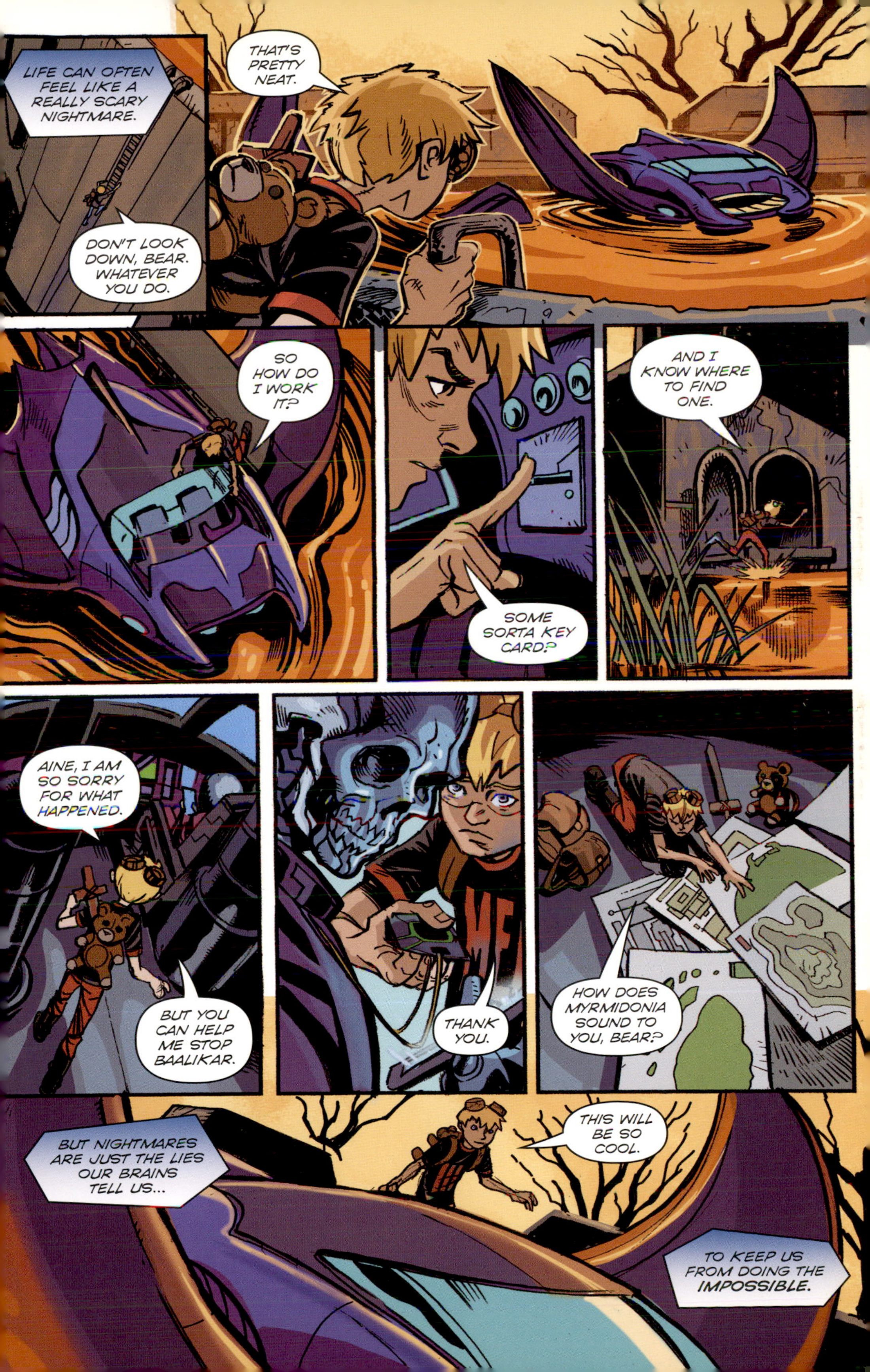
LIFE CAN OFTEN FEEL LIKE A REALLY SCARY NIGHTMARE.
DON'T LOOK DOWN, BEAR. WHATEVER YOU DO.
THAT'S PRETTY NEAT.
SO HOW DO I WORK IT?
SOME SORTA KEY CARD?
AND I KNOW WHERE TO FIND ONE.
AINE, I AM SO SORRY FOR WHAT HAPPENED.
BUT YOU CAN HELP ME STOP BAALIKAR.
THANK YOU.
HOW DOES MYRMIDONIA SOUND TO YOU, BEAR?
BUT NIGHTMARES ARE JUST THE LIES OUR BRAINS TELL US...
THIS WILL BE SO COOL.
TO KEEP US FROM DOING THE IMPOSSIBLE.

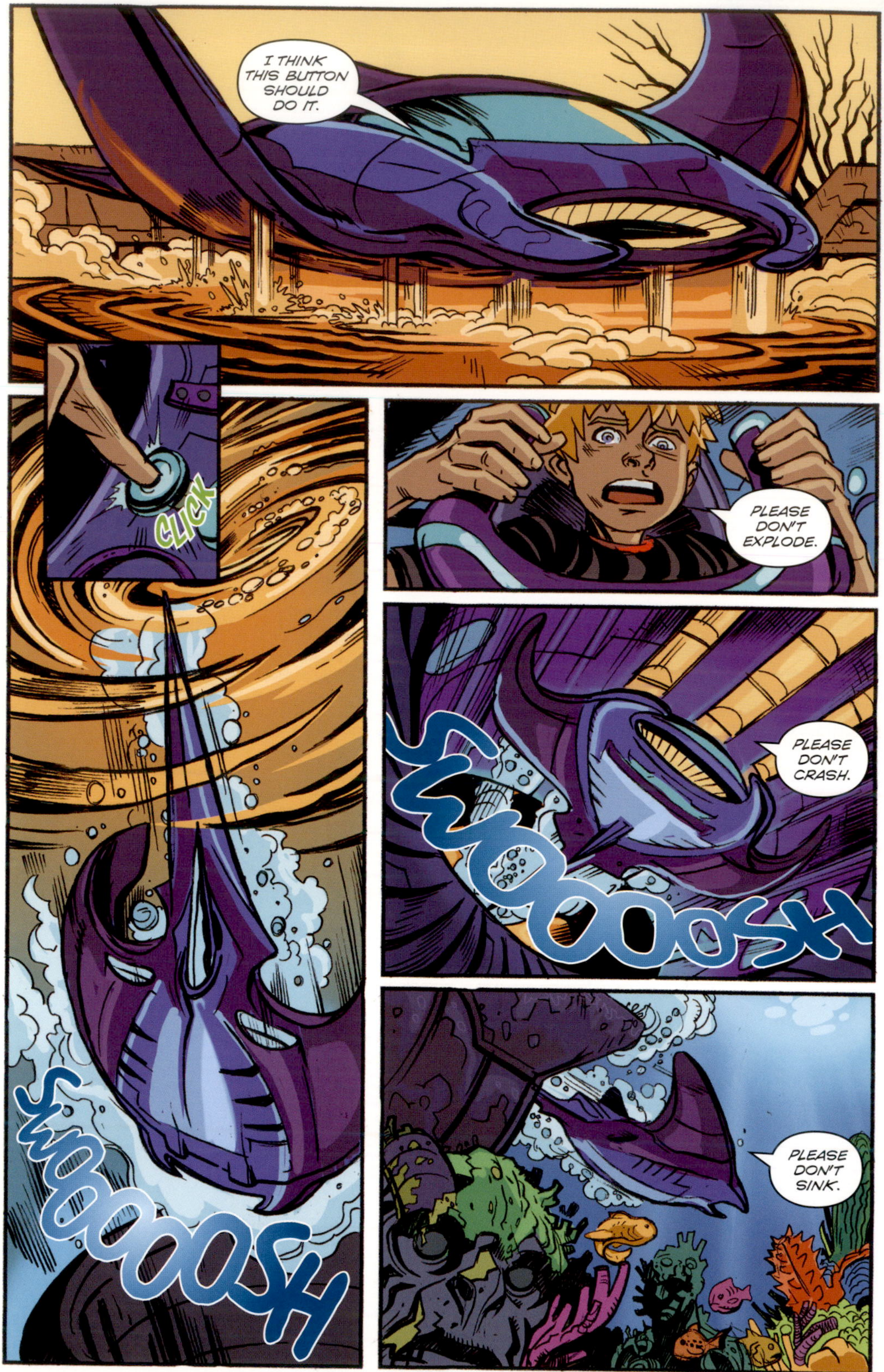
I THINK THIS BUTTON SHOULD DO IT.
CLICK
PLEASE DON'T EXPLODE.
PLEASE DON'T CRASH.
SWOOOOOSH
SWOOOOSH
PLEASE DON'T SINK.

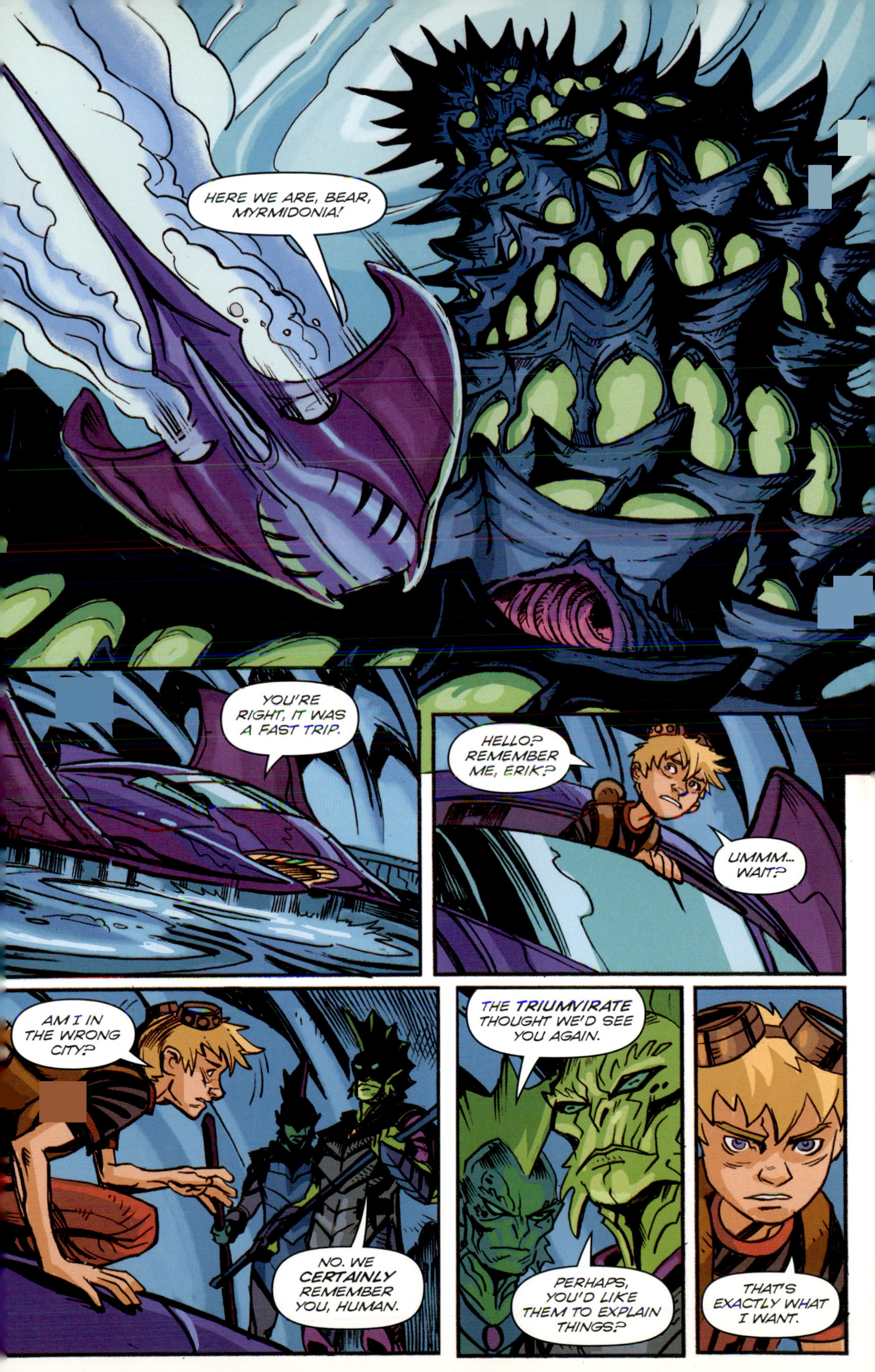
HERE WE ARE, BEAR, MYRMIDONIA!
YOU'RE RIGHT, IT WAS A FAST TRIP.
HELLO? REMEMBER ME, ERIK?
UMMM... WAIT?
AM I IN THE WRONG CITY?
NO. WE CERTAINLY REMEMBER YOU, HUMAN.
THE TRIUMVIRATE THOUGHT WE'D SEE YOU AGAIN.
PERHAPS, YOU'D LIKE THEM TO EXPLAIN THINGS?
THAT'S EXACTLY WHAT I WANT.

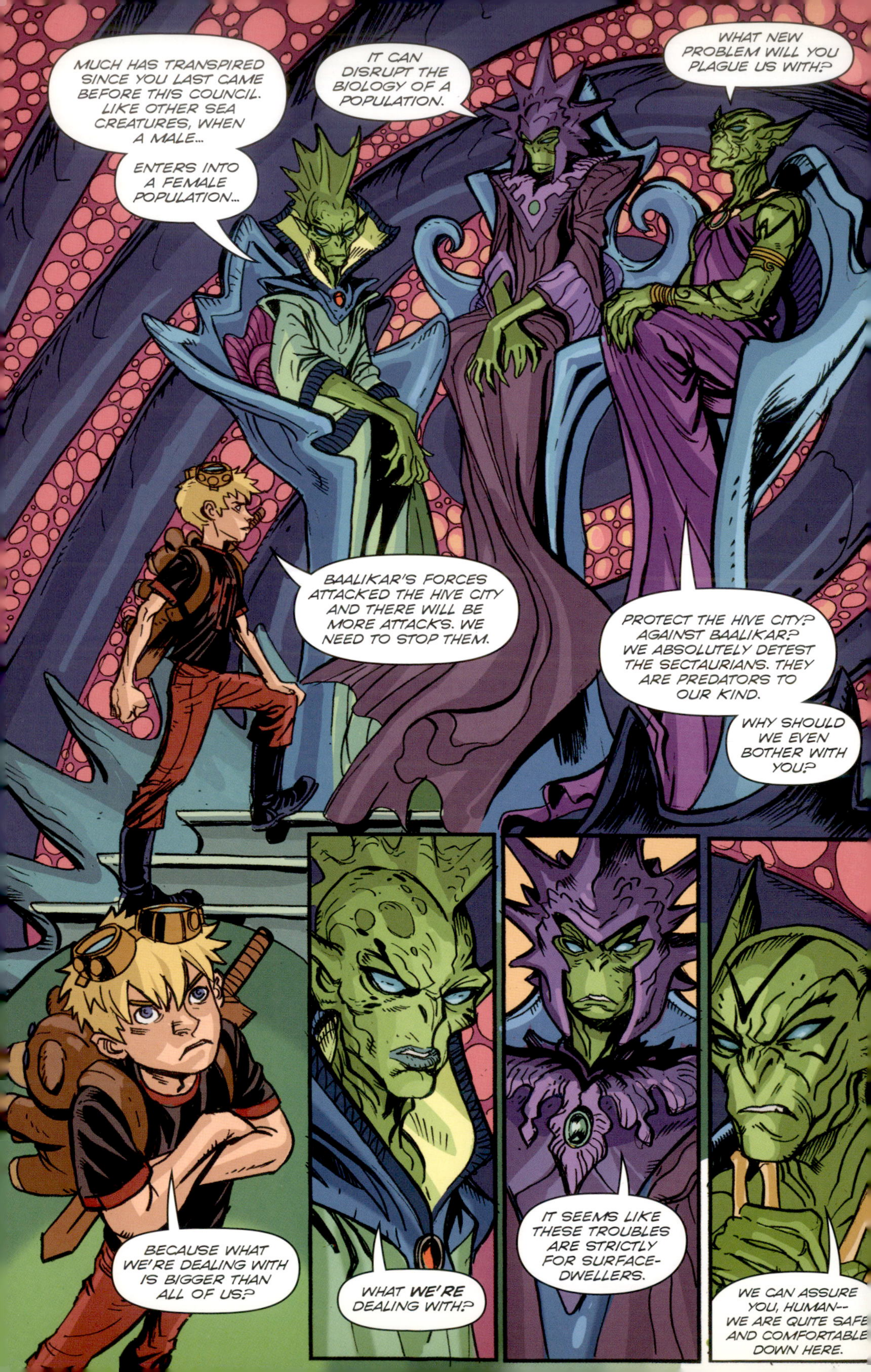
MUCH HAS TRANSPIRED SINCE YOU LAST CAME BEFORE THIS COUNCIL. LIKE OTHER SEA CREATURES, WHEN A MALE...
ENTERS INTO A FEMALE POPULATION...
IT CAN DISRUPT THE BIOLOGY OF A POPULATION.
WHAT NEW PROBLEM WILL YOU PLAGUE US WITH?
BAALIKAR'S FORCES ATTACKED THE HIVE CITY AND THERE WILL BE MORE ATTACKS. WE NEED TO STOP THEM.
PROTECT THE HIVE CITY? AGAINST BAALIKAR? WE ABSOLUTELY DETEST THE SECTAURIANS. THEY ARE PREDATORS TO OUR KIND.
WHY SHOULD WE EVEN BOTHER WITH YOU?
BECAUSE WHAT WE'RE DEALING WITH IS BIGGER THAN ALL OF US?
WHAT **WE'RE** DEALING WITH?
IT SEEMS LIKE THESE TROUBLES ARE STRICTLY FOR SURFACE-DWELLERS.
WE CAN ASSURE YOU, HUMAN-- WE ARE QUITE SAFE AND COMFORTABLE DOWN HERE.

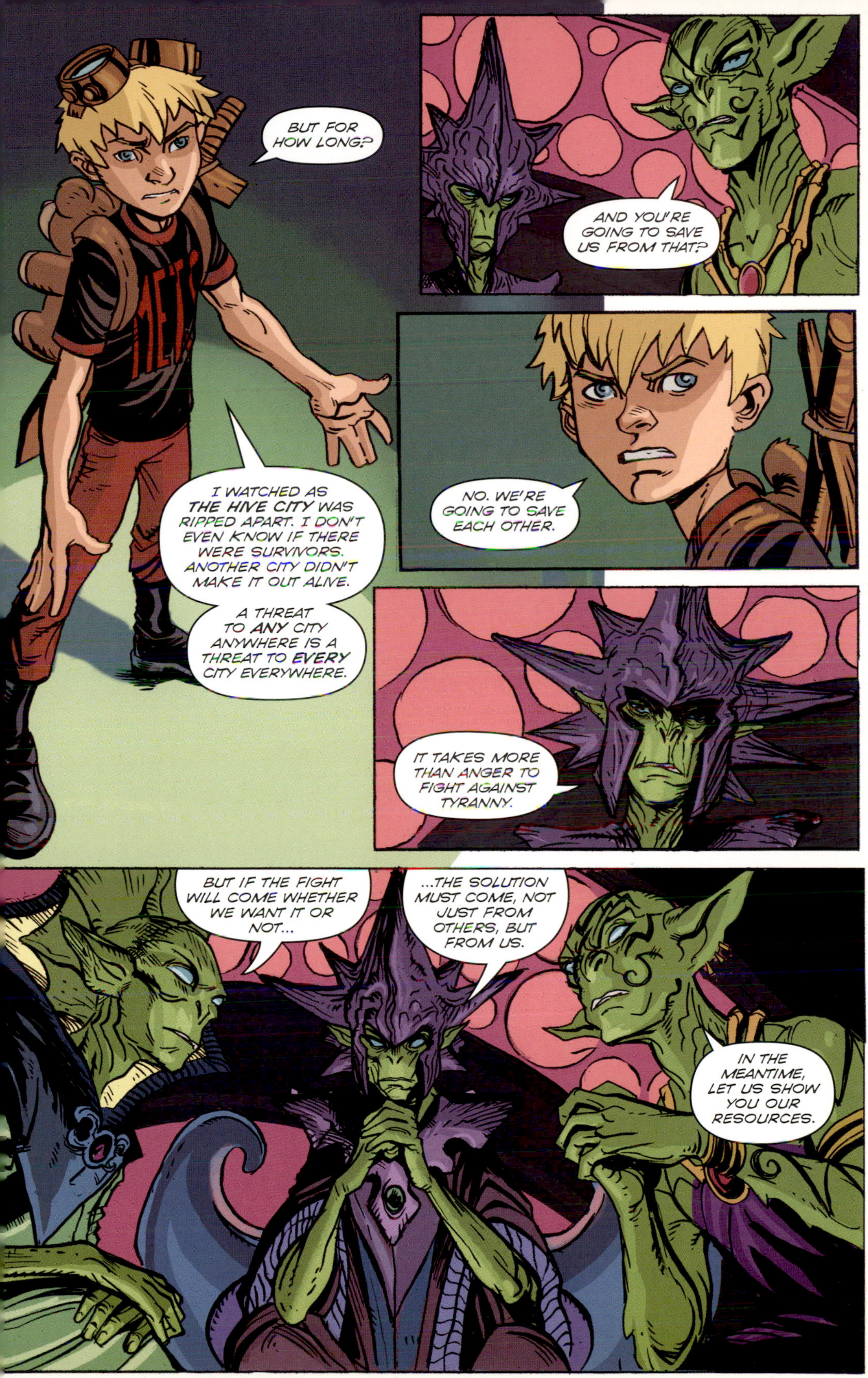
BUT FOR HOW LONG?
AND YOU'RE GOING TO SAVE US FROM THAT?
NO. WE'RE GOING TO SAVE EACH OTHER.
I WATCHED AS THE HIVE CITY WAS RIPPED APART. I DON'T EVEN KNOW IF THERE WERE SURVIVORS. ANOTHER CITY DIDN'T MAKE IT OUT ALIVE.
A THREAT TO ANY CITY ANYWHERE IS A THREAT TO EVERY CITY EVERYWHERE.
IT TAKES MORE THAN ANGER TO FIGHT AGAINST TYRANNY.
BUT IF THE FIGHT WILL COME WHETHER WE WANT IT OR NOT...
...THE SOLUTION MUST COME, NOT JUST FROM OTHERS, BUT FROM US.
IN THE MEANTIME, LET US SHOW YOU OUR RESOURCES.

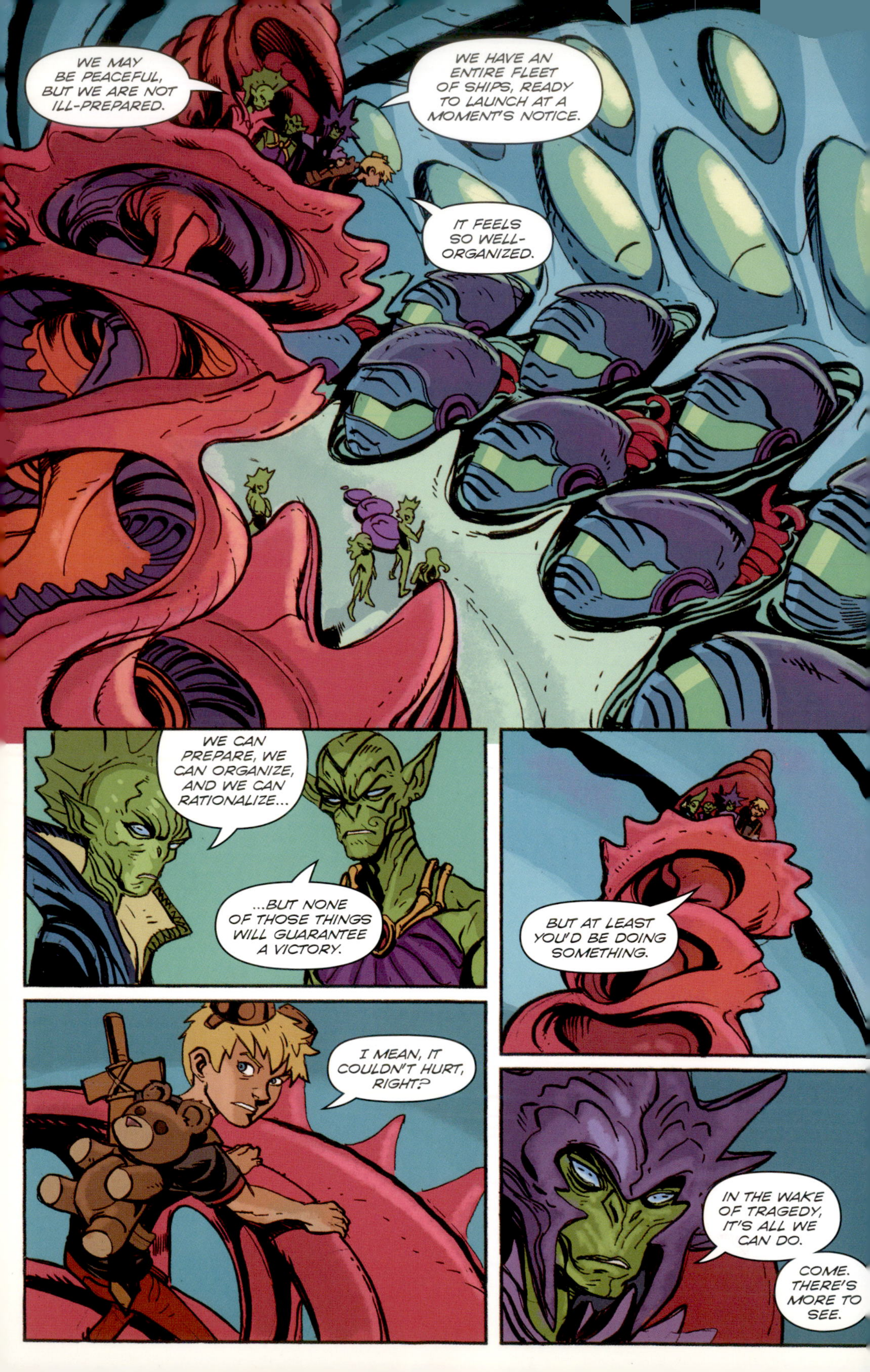
WE MAY BE PEACEFUL, BUT WE ARE NOT ILL-PREPARED.
WE HAVE AN ENTIRE FLEET OF SHIPS, READY TO LAUNCH AT A MOMENT'S NOTICE.
IT FEELS SO WELL-ORGANIZED.
WE CAN PREPARE, WE CAN ORGANIZE, AND WE CAN RATIONALIZE...
...BUT NONE OF THOSE THINGS WILL GUARANTEE A VICTORY.
BUT AT LEAST YOU'D BE DOING SOMETHING.
I MEAN, IT COULDN'T HURT, RIGHT?
IN THE WAKE OF TRAGEDY, IT'S ALL WE CAN DO.
COME. THERE'S MORE TO SEE.

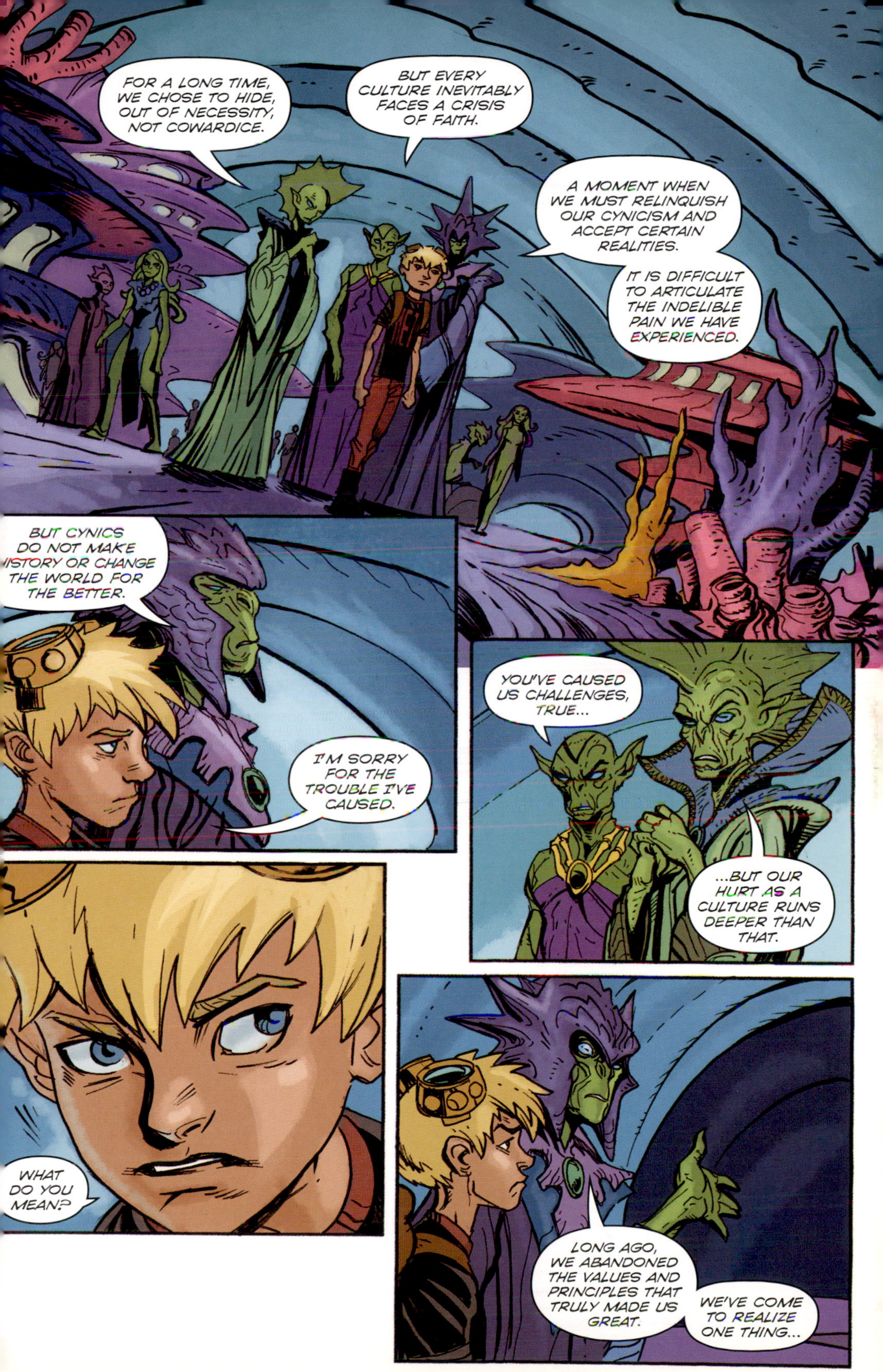
FOR A LONG TIME, WE CHOSE TO HIDE, OUT OF NECESSITY, NOT COWARDICE.
BUT EVERY CULTURE INEVITABLY FACES A CRISIS OF FAITH.
A MOMENT WHEN WE MUST RELINQUISH OUR CYNICISM AND ACCEPT CERTAIN REALITIES.
IT IS DIFFICULT TO ARTICULATE THE INDELIBLE PAIN WE HAVE EXPERIENCED.
BUT CYNICS DO NOT MAKE HISTORY OR CHANGE THE WORLD FOR THE BETTER.
I'M SORRY FOR THE TROUBLE I'VE CAUSED.
YOU'VE CAUSED US CHALLENGES, TRUE...
...BUT OUR HURT AS A CULTURE RUNS DEEPER THAN THAT.
WHAT DO YOU MEAN?
LONG AGO, WE ABANDONED THE VALUES AND PRINCIPLES THAT TRULY MADE US GREAT.
WE'VE COME TO REALIZE ONE THING...

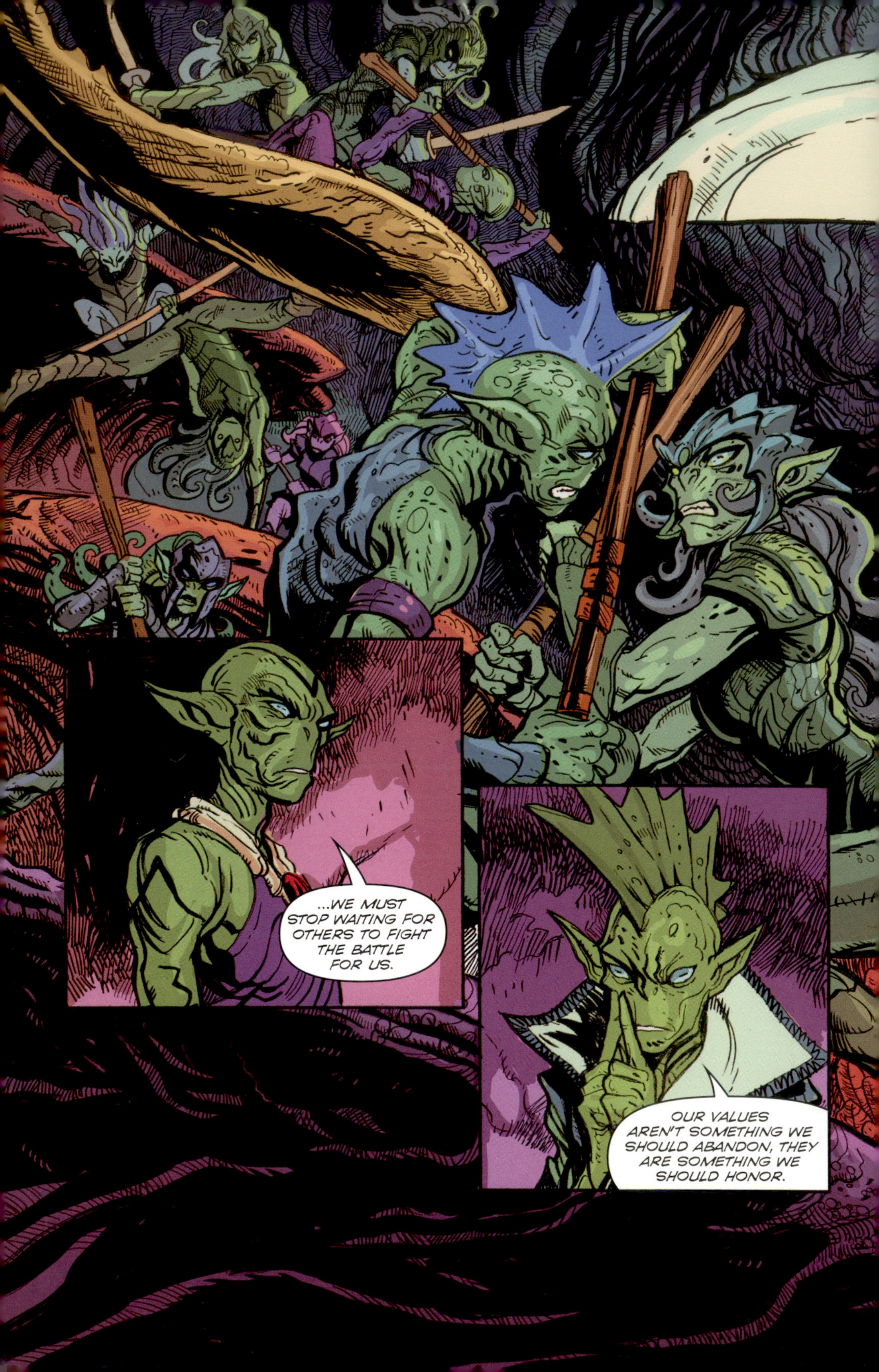
...WE MUST STOP WAITING FOR OTHERS TO FIGHT THE BATTLE FOR US.
OUR VALUES AREN'T SOMETHING WE SHOULD ABANDON, THEY ARE SOMETHING WE SHOULD HONOR.

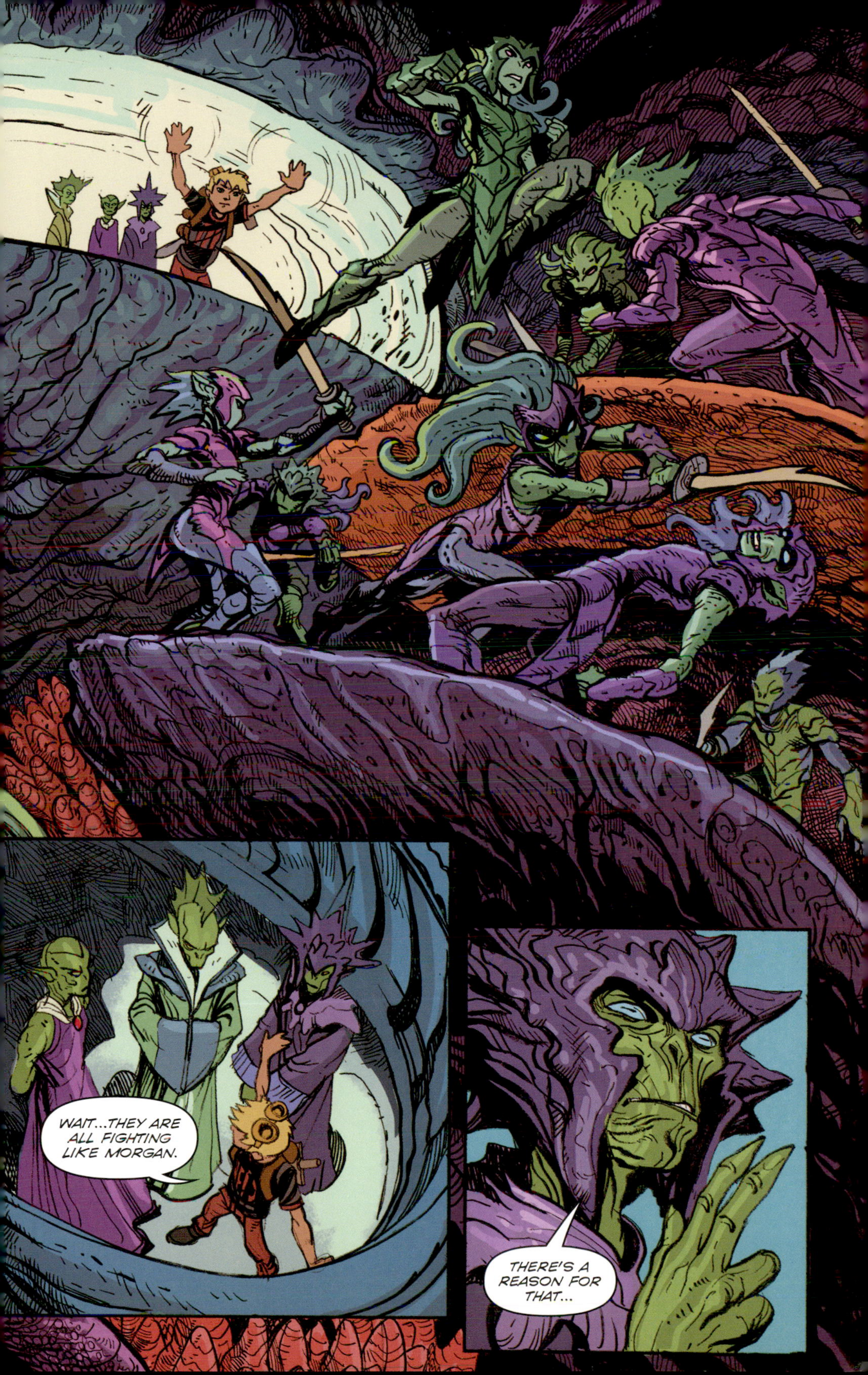
WAIT...THEY ARE ALL FIGHTING LIKE MORGAN.
THERE'S A REASON FOR THAT...

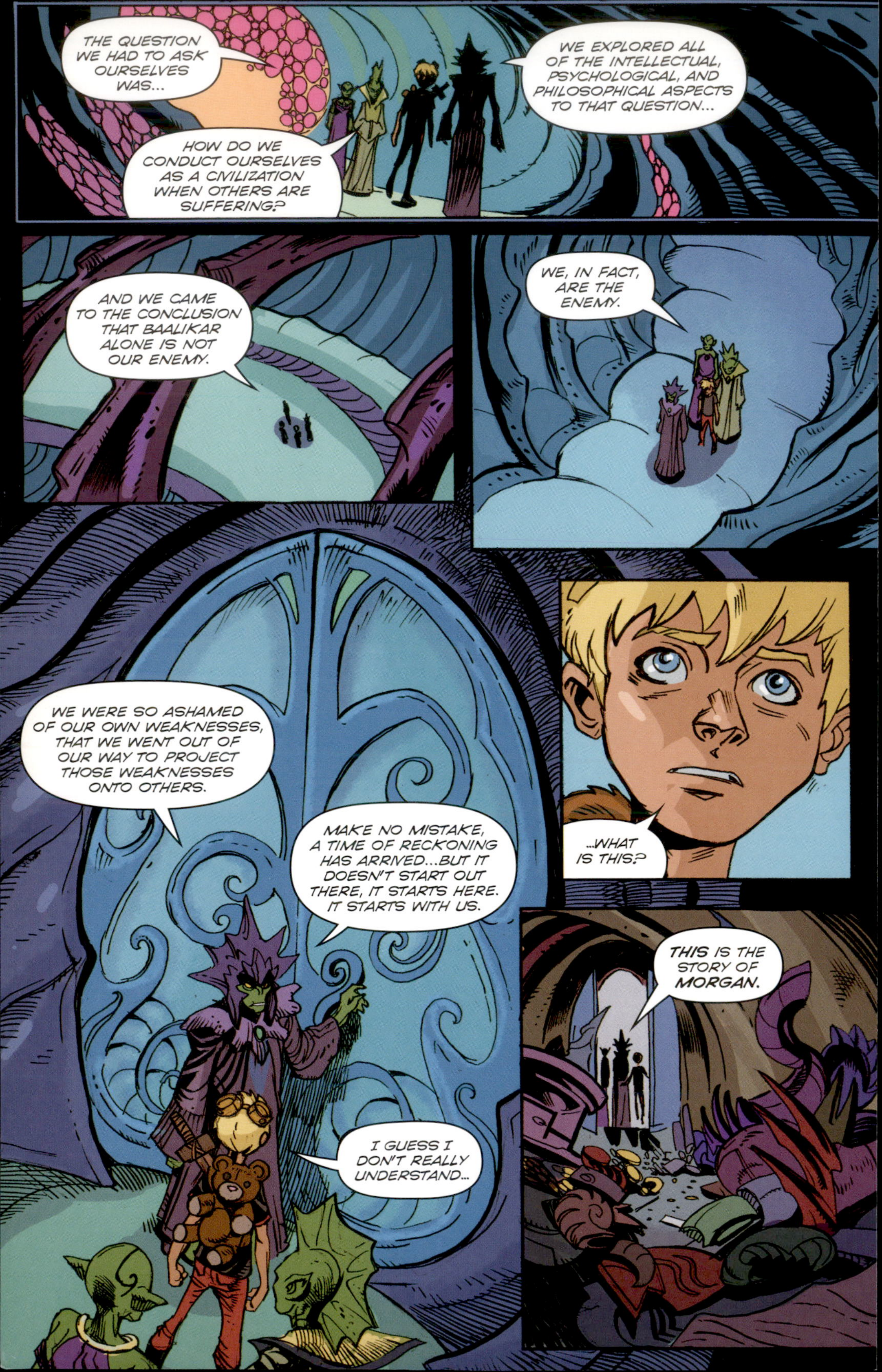
THE QUESTION WE HAD TO ASK OURSELVES WAS...
HOW DO WE CONDUCT OURSELVES AS A CIVILIZATION WHEN OTHERS ARE SUFFERING?
WE EXPLORED ALL OF THE INTELLECTUAL, PSYCHOLOGICAL, AND PHILOSOPHICAL ASPECTS TO THAT QUESTION...
AND WE CAME TO THE CONCLUSION THAT BAALIKAR ALONE IS NOT OUR ENEMY.
WE, IN FACT, ARE THE ENEMY.
WE WERE SO ASHAMED OF OUR OWN WEAKNESSES, THAT WE WENT OUT OF OUR WAY TO PROJECT THOSE WEAKNESSES ONTO OTHERS.
MAKE NO MISTAKE, A TIME OF RECKONING HAS ARRIVED...BUT IT DOESN'T START OUT THERE, IT STARTS HERE. IT STARTS WITH US.
I GUESS I DON'T REALLY UNDERSTAND...
...WHAT IS THIS?
THIS IS THE STORY OF MORGAN.

CHAPTER EIGHT

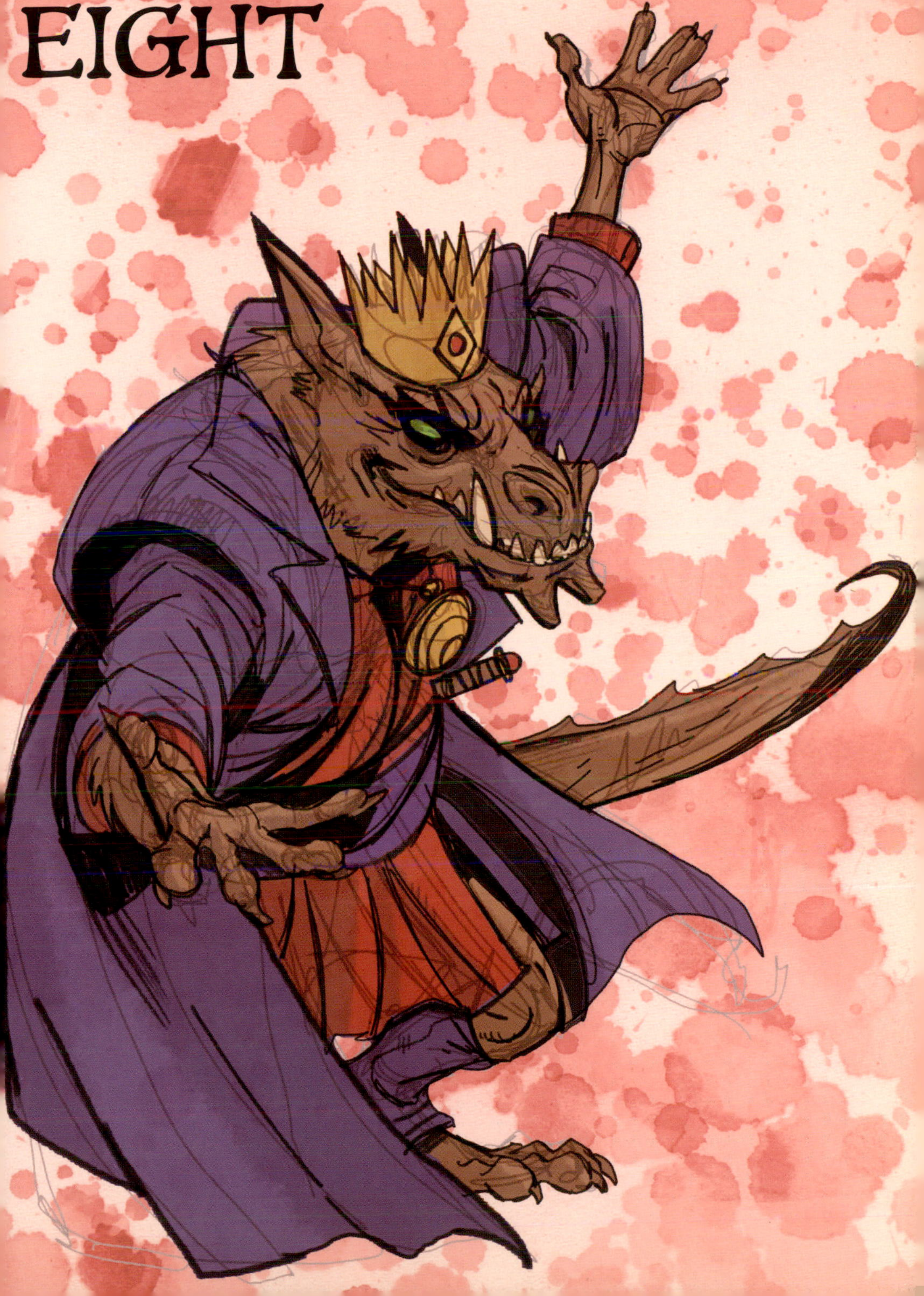

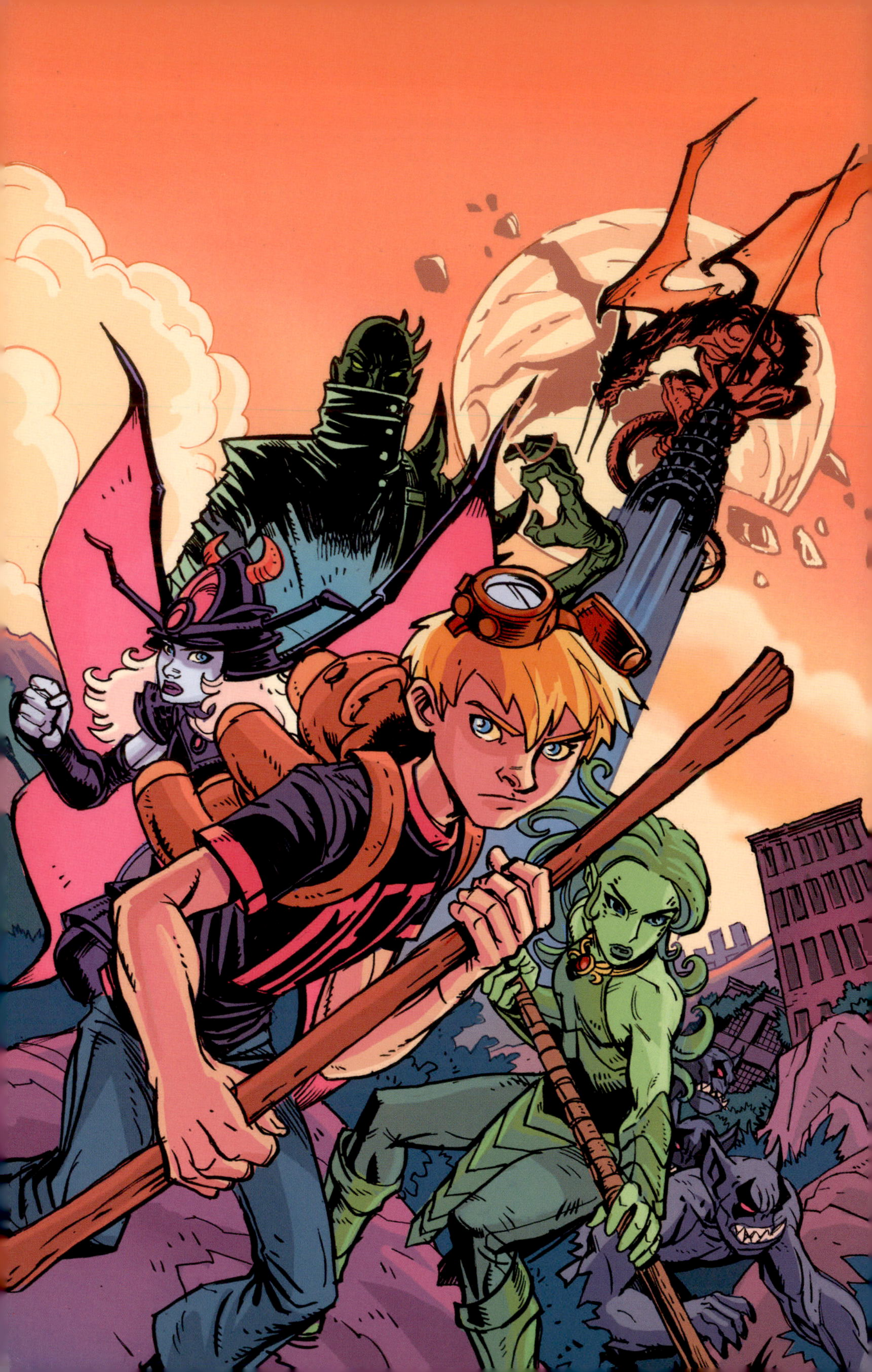

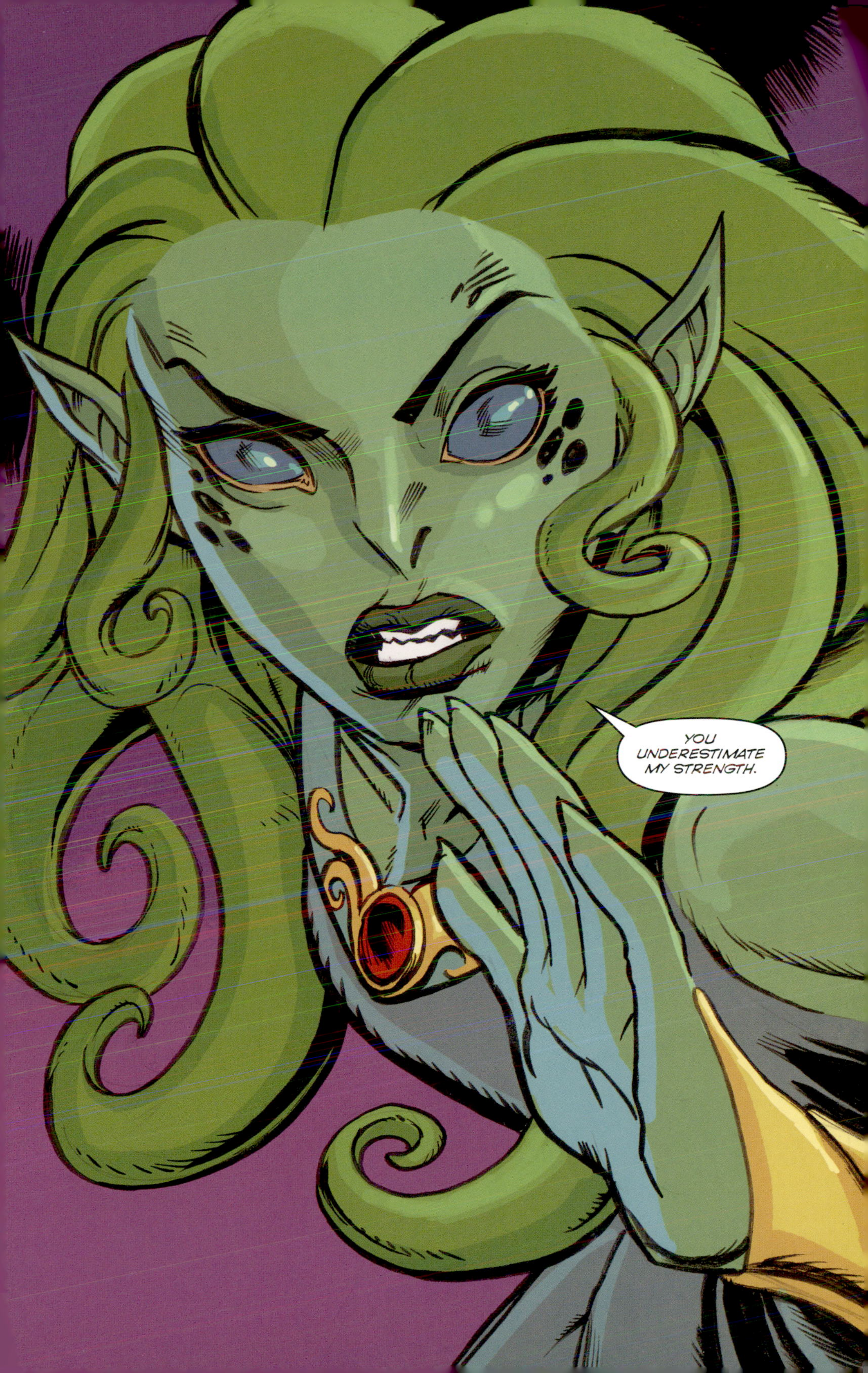
YOU UNDERESTIMATE MY STRENGTH.

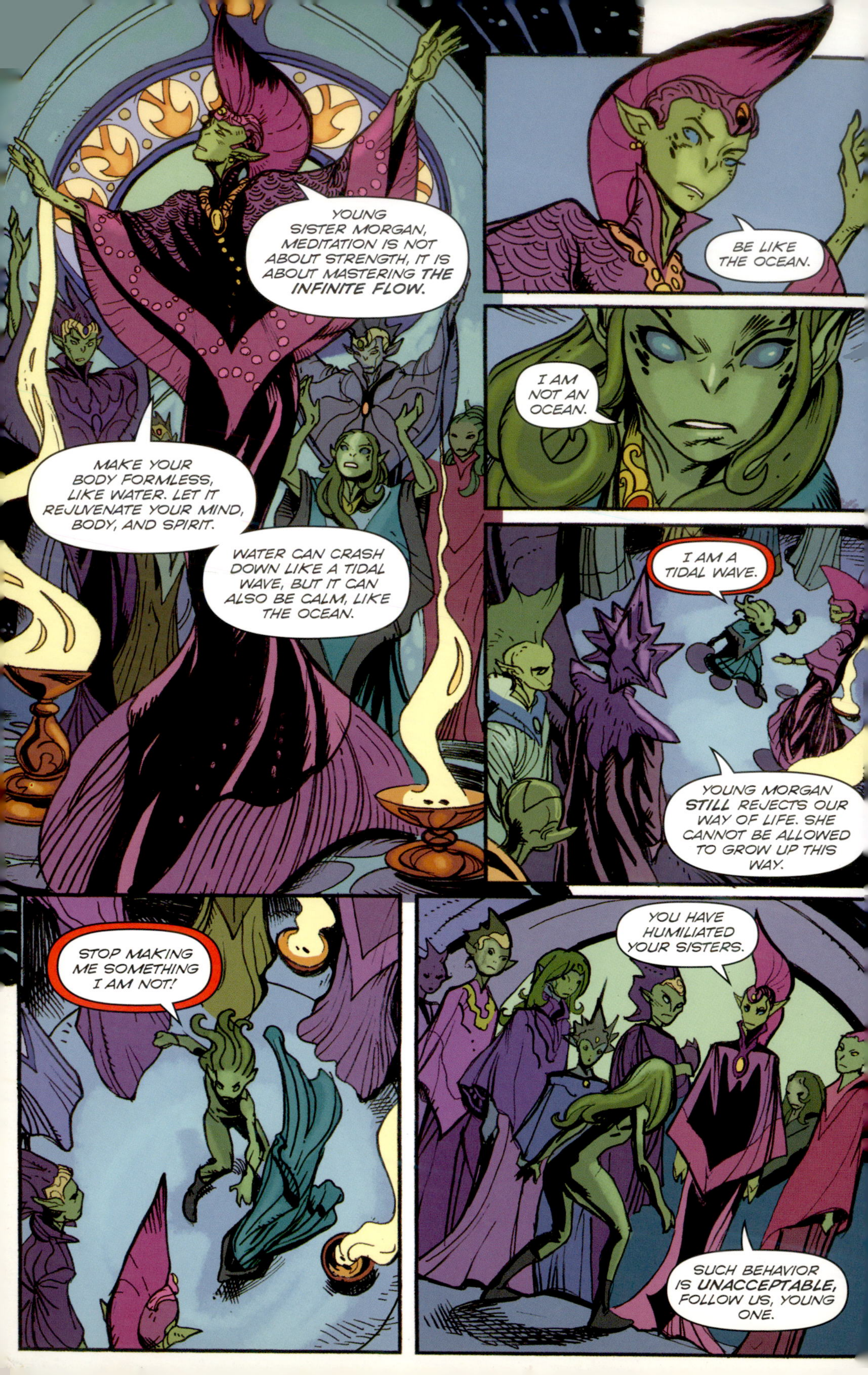
YOUNG SISTER MORGAN, MEDITATION IS NOT ABOUT STRENGTH, IT IS ABOUT MASTERING THE INFINITE FLOW.
MAKE YOUR BODY FORMLESS, LIKE WATER. LET IT REJUVENATE YOUR MIND, BODY, AND SPIRIT.
WATER CAN CRASH DOWN LIKE A TIDAL WAVE, BUT IT CAN ALSO BE CALM, LIKE THE OCEAN.
BE LIKE THE OCEAN.
I AM NOT AN OCEAN.
I AM A TIDAL WAVE.
YOUNG MORGAN STILL REJECTS OUR WAY OF LIFE. SHE CANNOT BE ALLOWED TO GROW UP THIS WAY.
STOP MAKING ME SOMETHING I AM NOT!
YOU HAVE HUMILIATED YOUR SISTERS.
SUCH BEHAVIOR IS UNACCEPTABLE, FOLLOW US, YOUNG ONE.

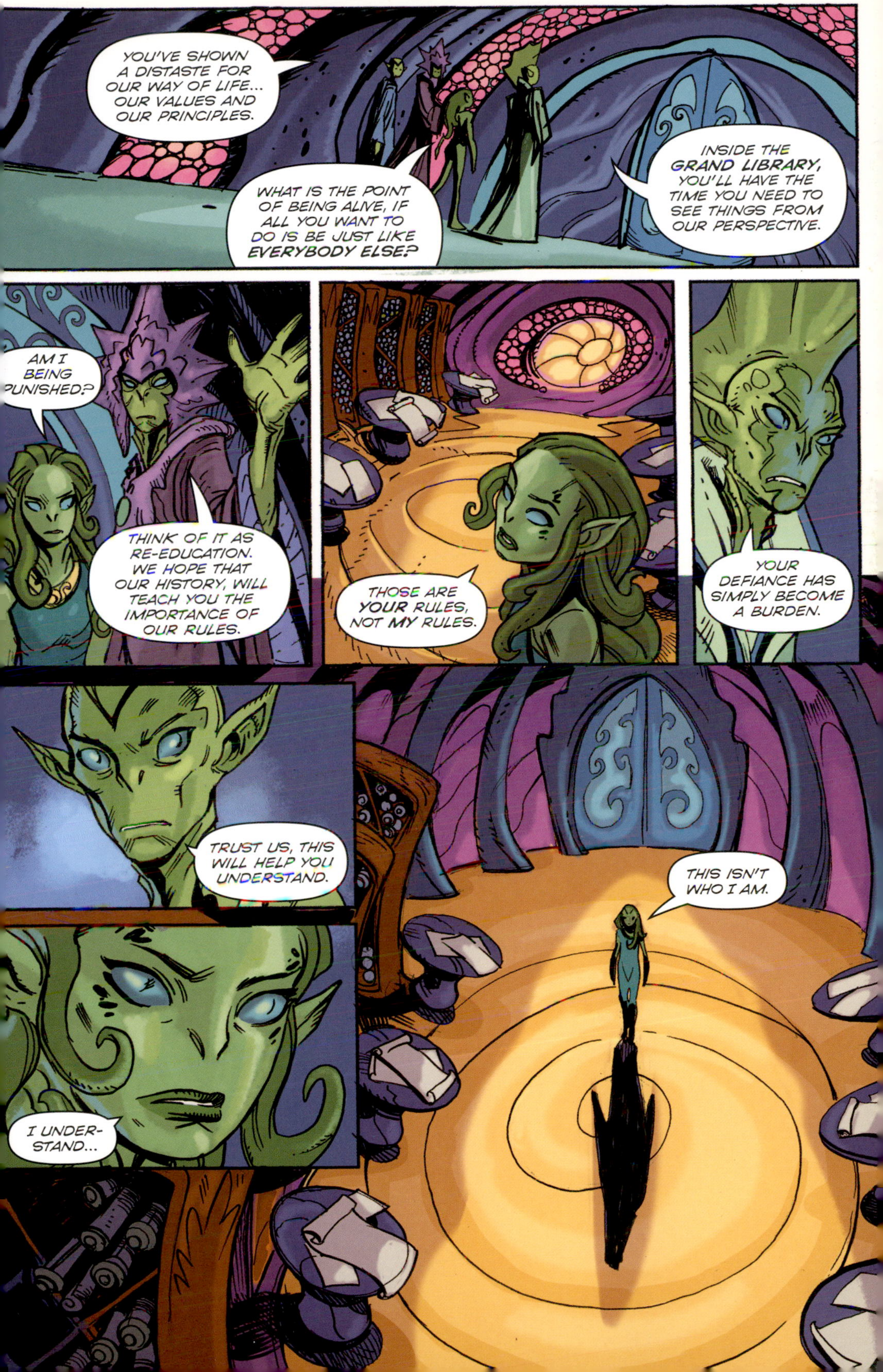
YOU'VE SHOWN A DISTASTE FOR OUR WAY OF LIFE... OUR VALUES AND OUR PRINCIPLES.
WHAT IS THE POINT OF BEING ALIVE, IF ALL YOU WANT TO DO IS BE JUST LIKE EVERYBODY ELSE?
INSIDE THE GRAND LIBRARY, YOU'LL HAVE THE TIME YOU NEED TO SEE THINGS FROM OUR PERSPECTIVE.
AM I BEING PUNISHED?
THINK OF IT AS RE-EDUCATION. WE HOPE THAT OUR HISTORY, WILL TEACH YOU THE IMPORTANCE OF OUR RULES.
THOSE ARE YOUR RULES, NOT MY RULES.
YOUR DEFIANCE HAS SIMPLY BECOME A BURDEN.
TRUST US, THIS WILL HELP YOU UNDERSTAND.
I UNDER-STAND...
THIS ISN'T WHO I AM.

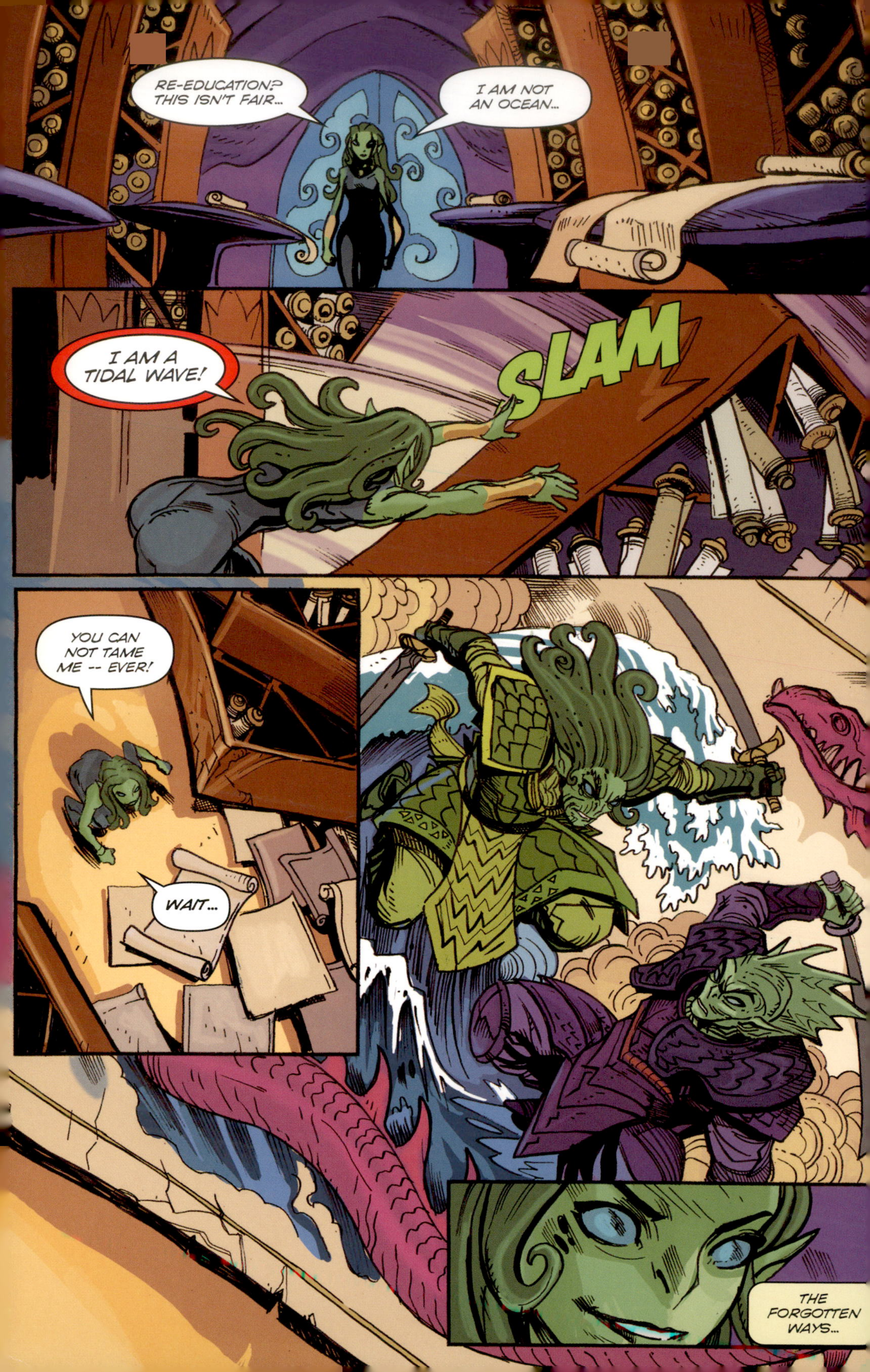

RE-EDUCATION? THIS ISN'T FAIR...
I AM NOT AN OCEAN...
I AM A TIDAL WAVE!
SLAM
YOU CAN NOT TAME ME -- EVER!
WAIT...
THE FORGOTTEN WAYS...

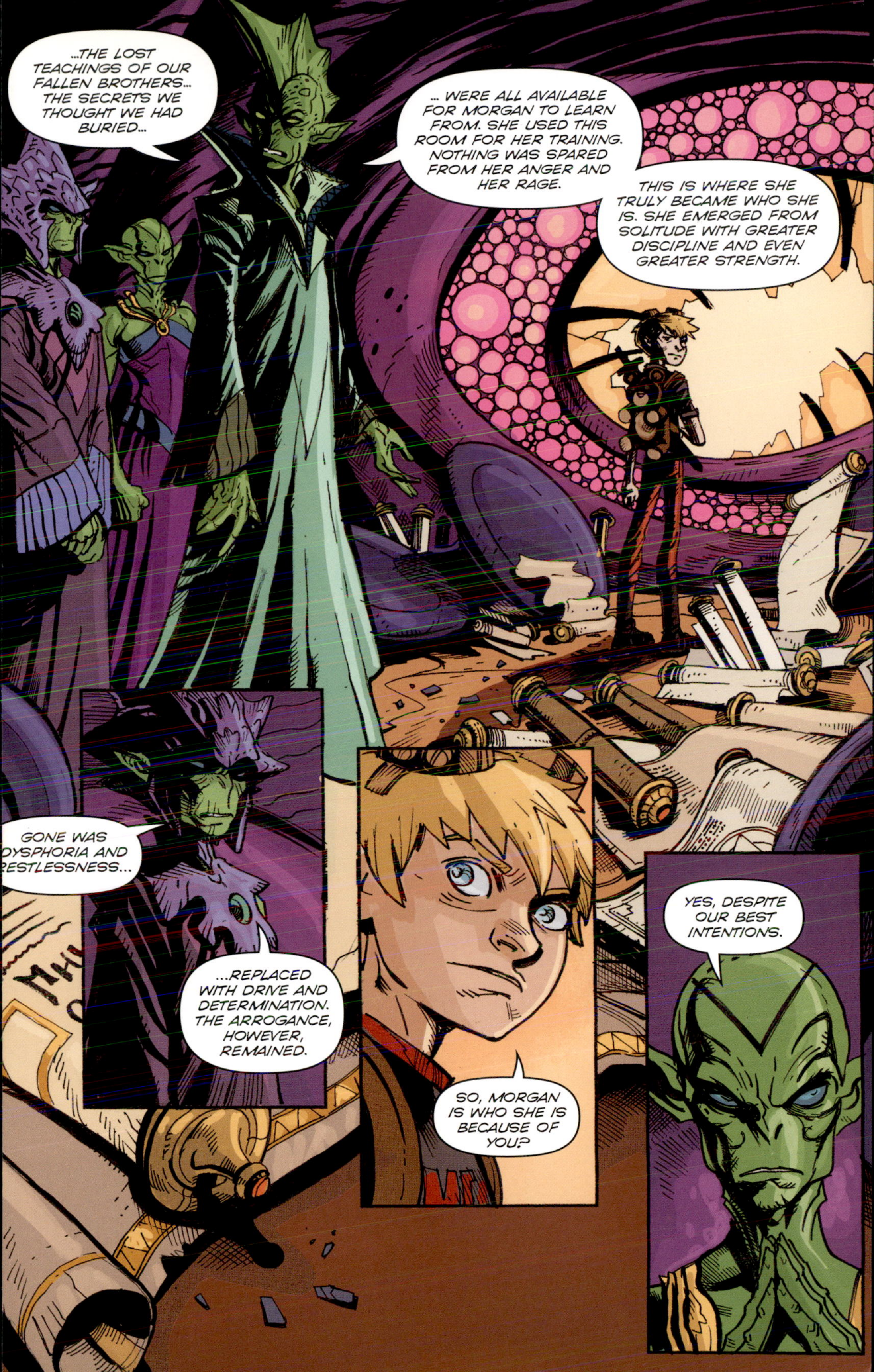
...THE LOST TEACHINGS OF OUR FALLEN BROTHERS... THE SECRETS WE THOUGHT WE HAD BURIED...
... WERE ALL AVAILABLE FOR MORGAN TO LEARN FROM. SHE USED THIS ROOM FOR HER TRAINING. NOTHING WAS SPARED FROM HER ANGER AND HER RAGE.
THIS IS WHERE SHE TRULY BECAME WHO SHE IS. SHE EMERGED FROM SOLITUDE WITH GREATER DISCIPLINE AND EVEN GREATER STRENGTH.
GONE WAS DYSPHORIA AND RESTLESSNESS...
...REPLACED WITH DRIVE AND DETERMINATION. THE ARROGANCE, HOWEVER, REMAINED.
SO, MORGAN IS WHO SHE IS BECAUSE OF YOU?
YES, DESPITE OUR BEST INTENTIONS.

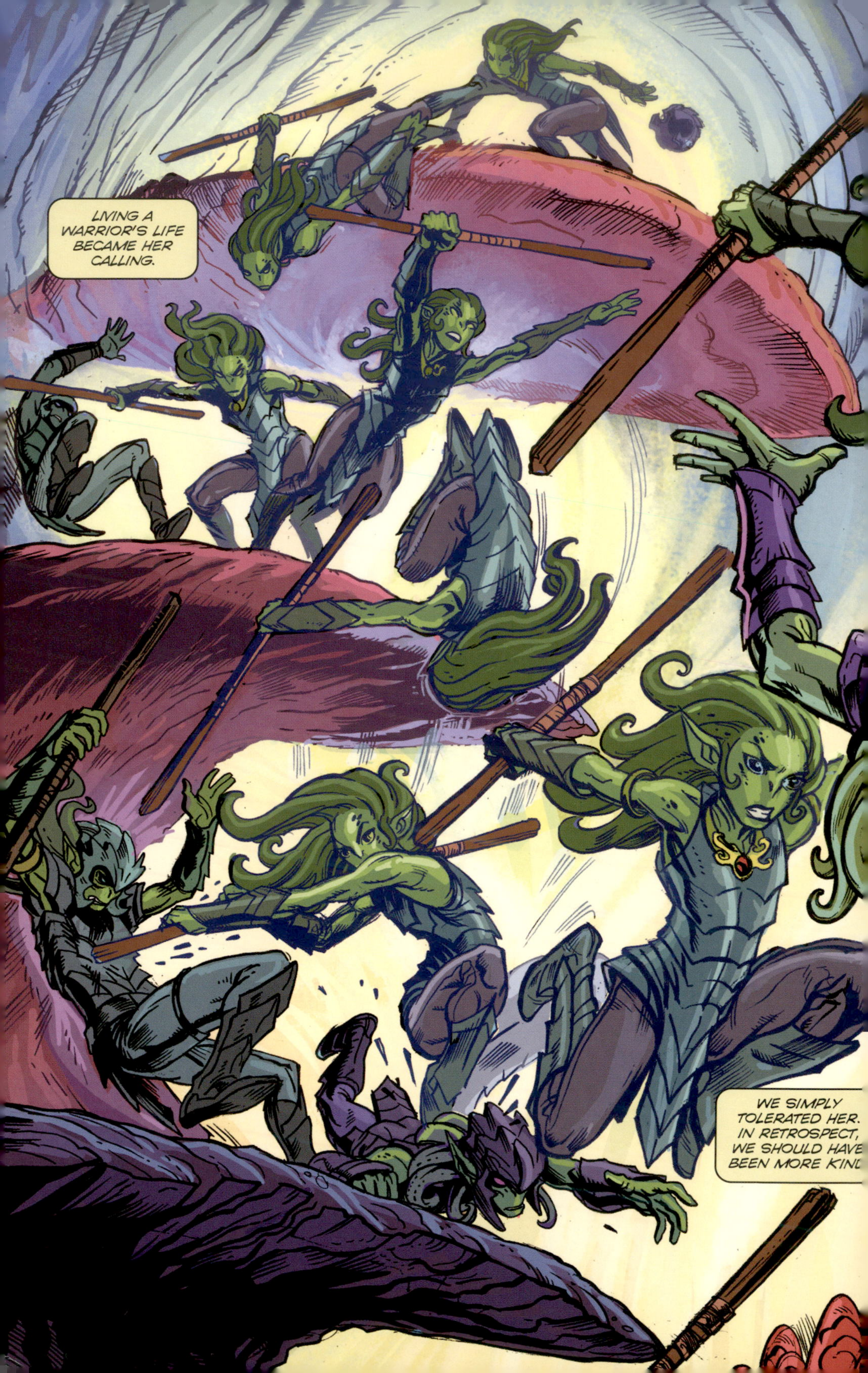
LIVING A WARRIOR'S LIFE BECAME HER CALLING.
WE SIMPLY TOLERATED HER. IN RETROSPECT, WE SHOULD HAVE BEEN MORE KIND

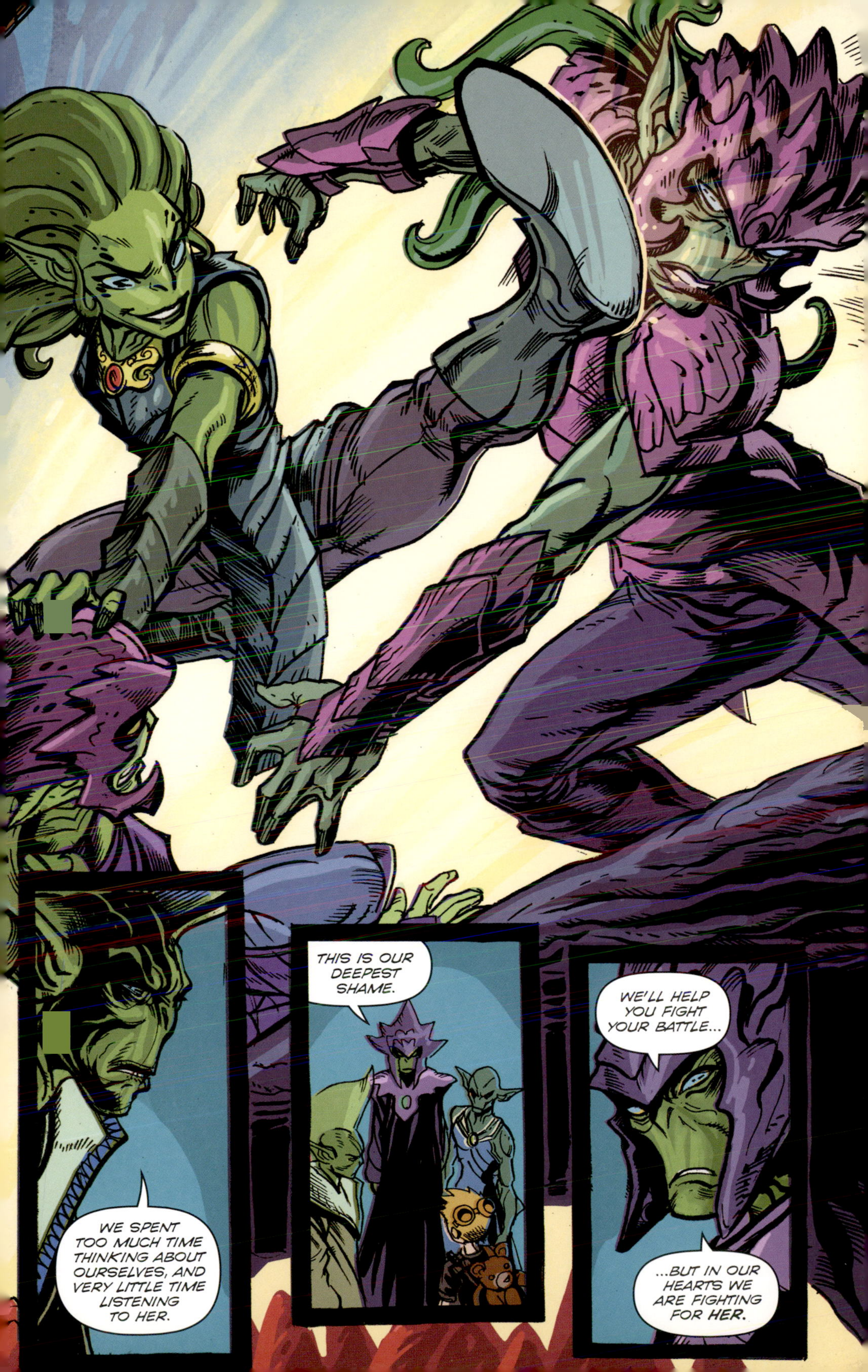
WE SPENT TOO MUCH TIME THINKING ABOUT OURSELVES, AND VERY LITTLE TIME LISTENING TO HER.
THIS IS OUR DEEPEST SHAME.
WE'LL HELP YOU FIGHT YOUR BATTLE...
...BUT IN OUR HEARTS WE ARE FIGHTING FOR HER.

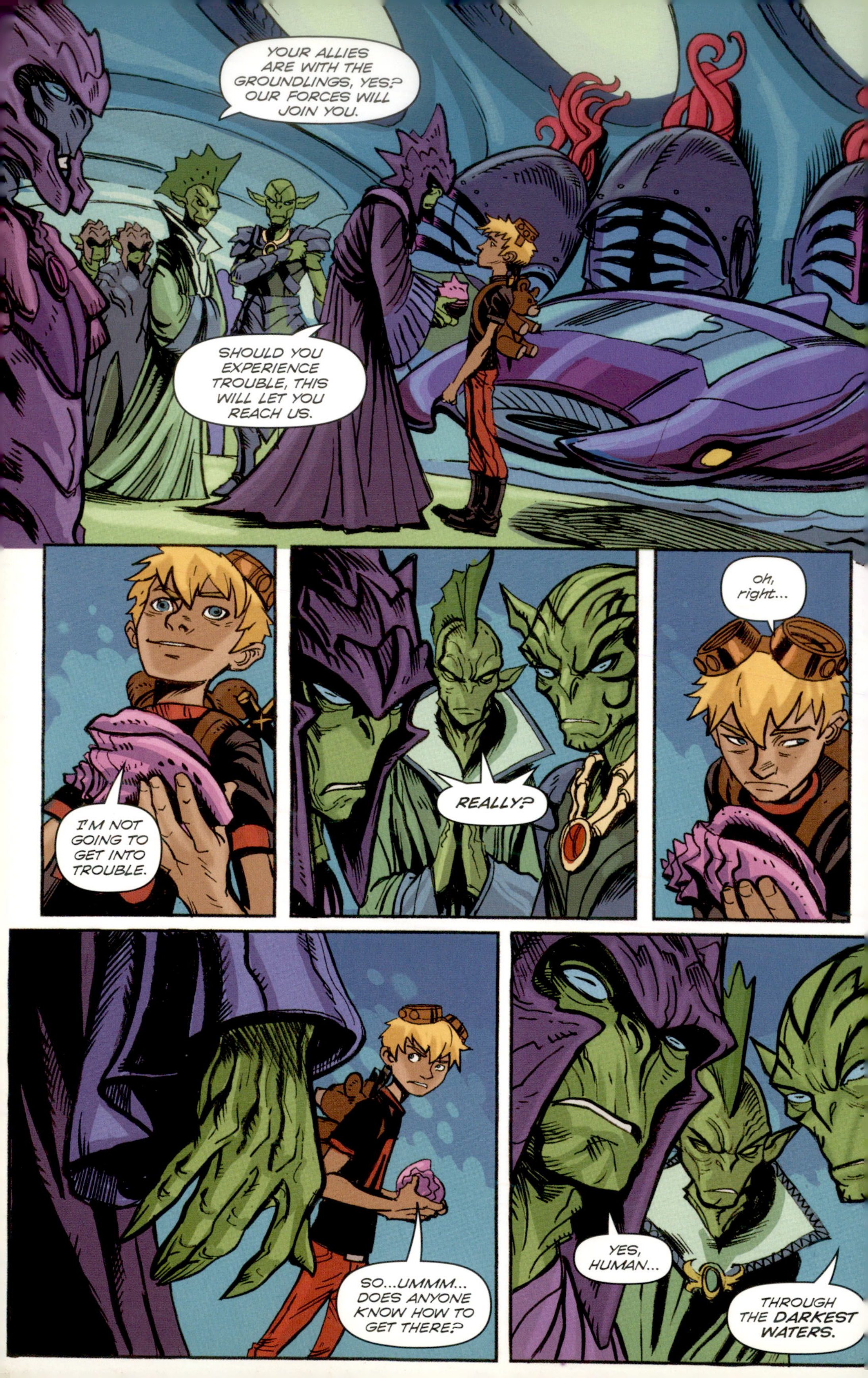

YOUR ALLIES ARE WITH THE GROUNDLINGS, YES? OUR FORCES WILL JOIN YOU.
SHOULD YOU EXPERIENCE TROUBLE, THIS WILL LET YOU REACH US.
I'M NOT GOING TO GET INTO TROUBLE.
REALLY?
oh, right...
SO...UMMM... DOES ANYONE KNOW HOW TO GET THERE?
YES, HUMAN...
THROUGH THE DARKEST WATERS.

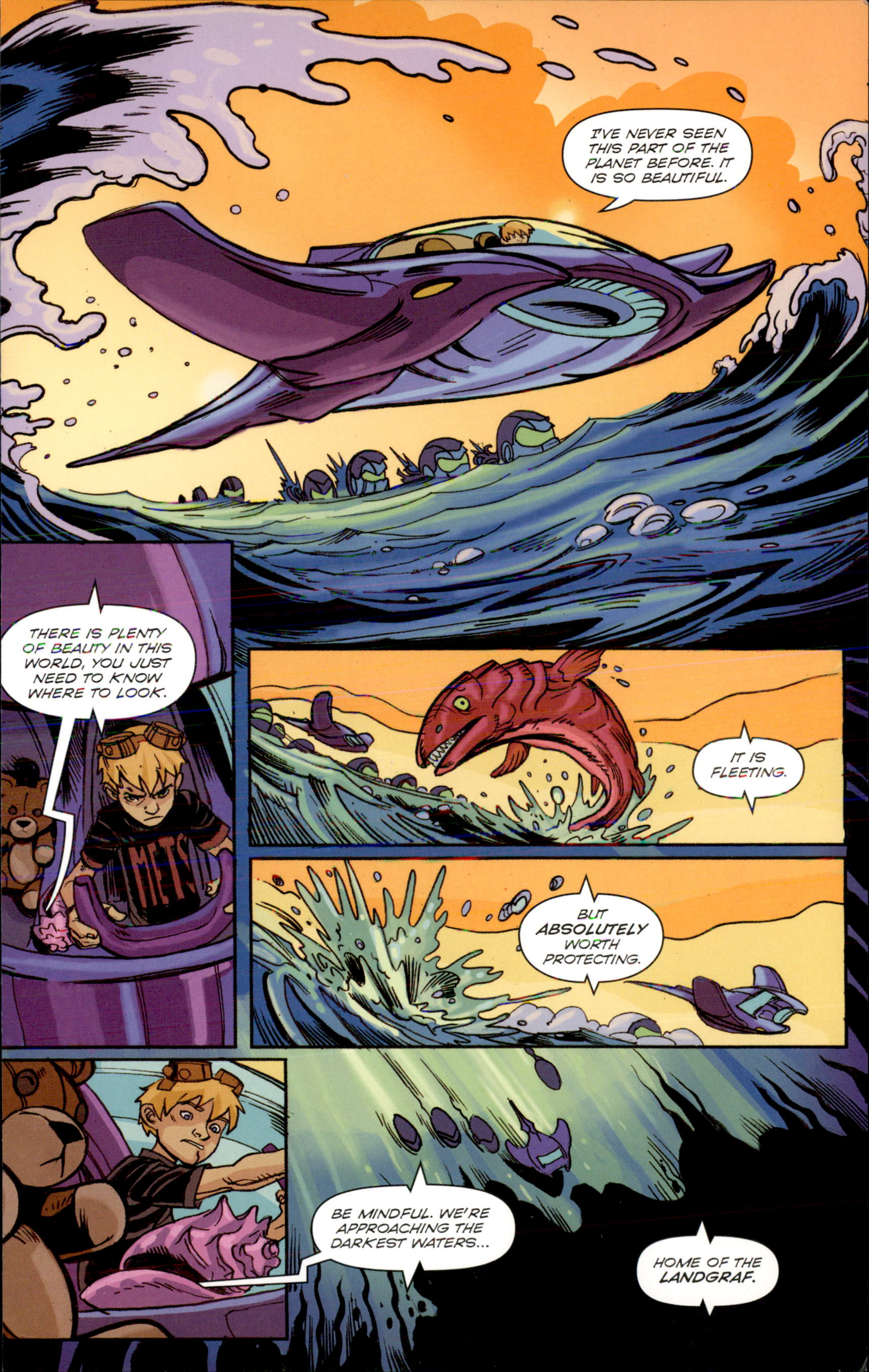

I'VE NEVER SEEN THIS PART OF THE PLANET BEFORE. IT IS SO BEAUTIFUL.
THERE IS PLENTY OF BEAUTY IN THIS WORLD, YOU JUST NEED TO KNOW WHERE TO LOOK.
IT IS FLEETING.
BUT ABSOLUTELY WORTH PROTECTING.
BE MINDFUL. WE'RE APPROACHING THE DARKEST WATERS...
HOME OF THE LANDGRAF.

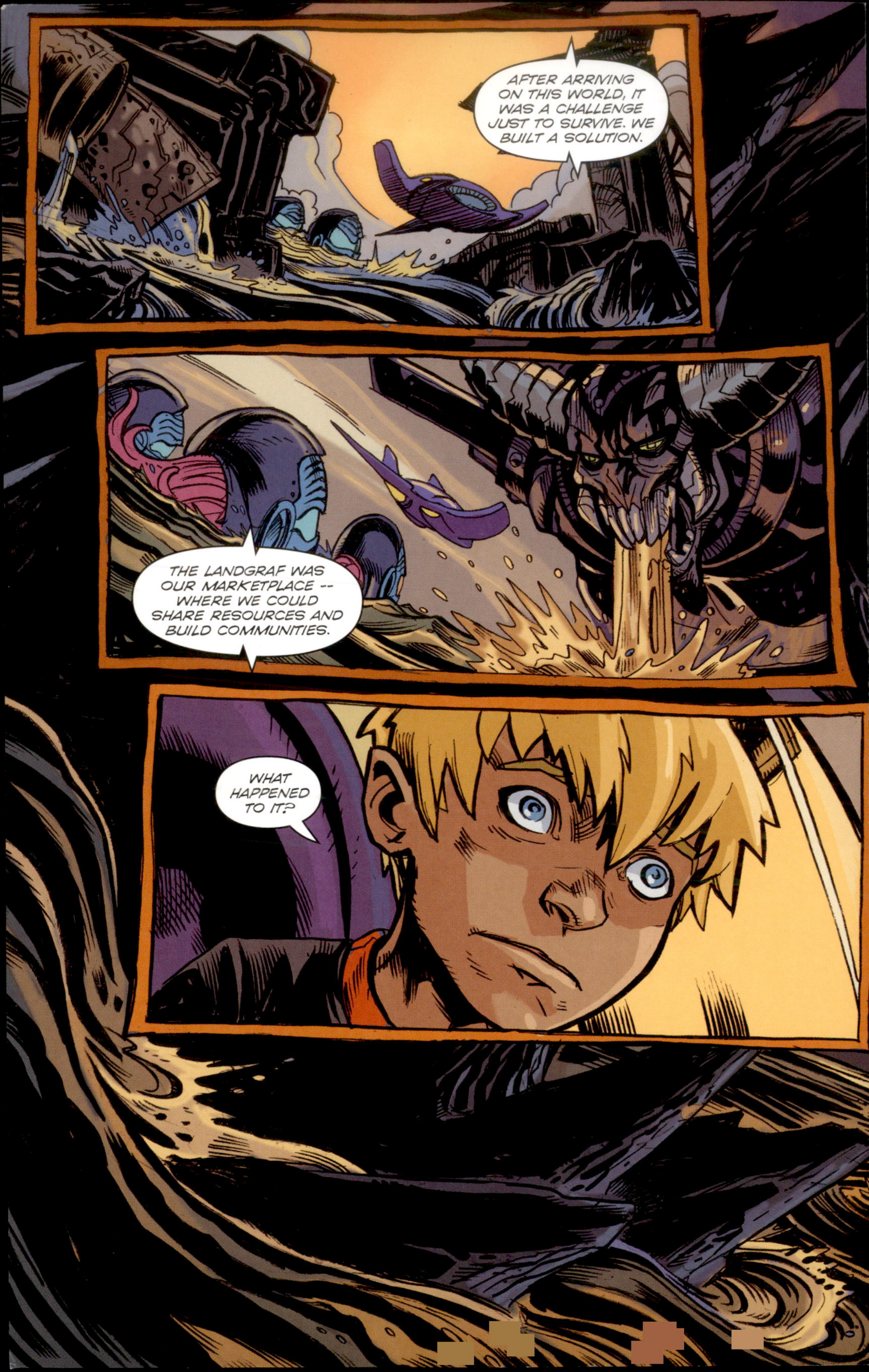
AFTER ARRIVING ON THIS WORLD, IT WAS A CHALLENGE JUST TO SURVIVE. WE BUILT A SOLUTION.
THE LANDGRAF WAS OUR MARKETPLACE -- WHERE WE COULD SHARE RESOURCES AND BUILD COMMUNITIES.
WHAT HAPPENED TO IT?

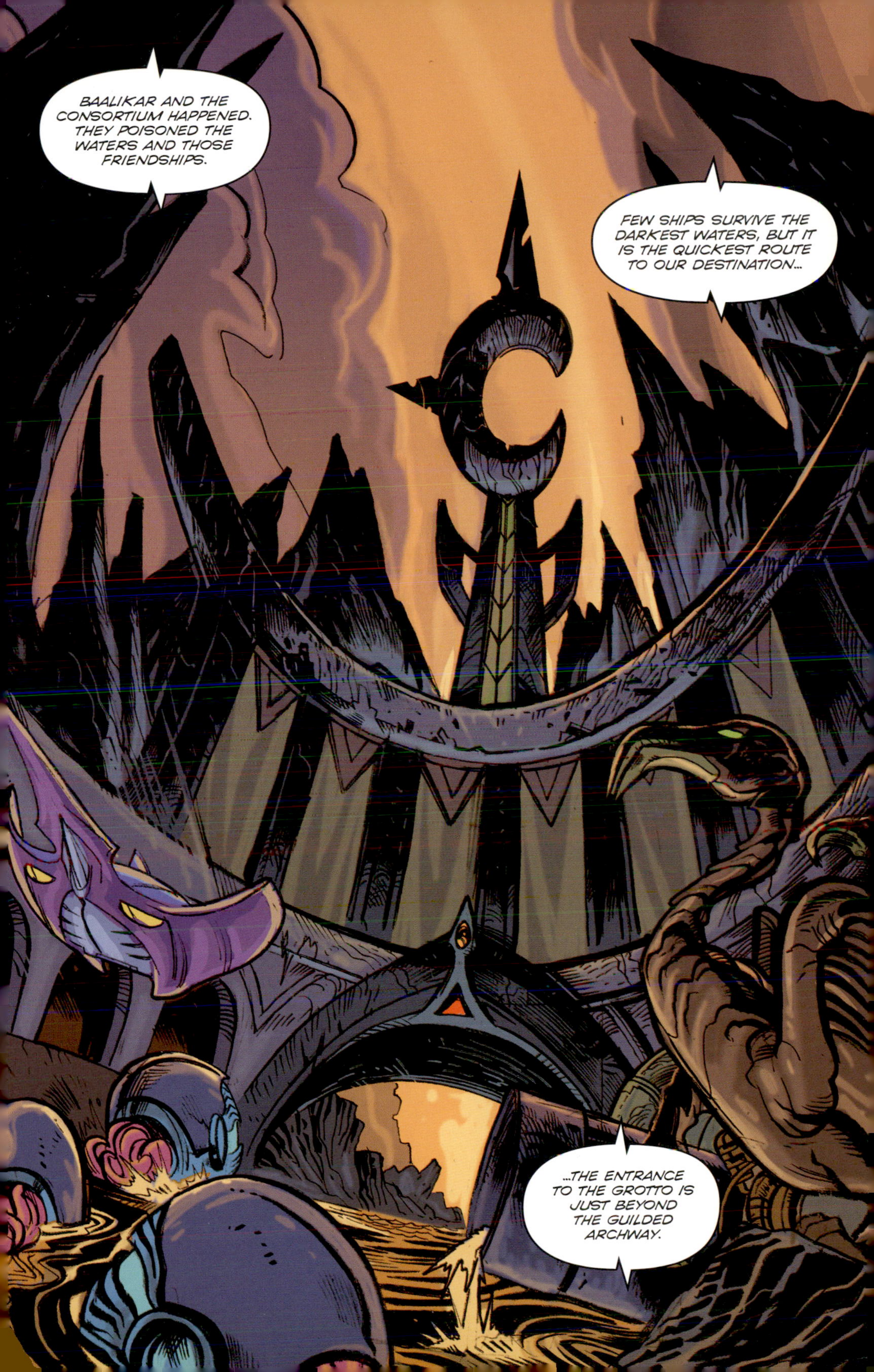
BAALIKAR AND THE CONSORTIUM HAPPENED. THEY POISONED THE WATERS AND THOSE FRIENDSHIPS.
FEW SHIPS SURVIVE THE DARKEST WATERS, BUT IT IS THE QUICKEST ROUTE TO OUR DESTINATION...
...THE ENTRANCE TO THE GROTTO IS JUST BEYOND THE GUILDED ARCHWAY.

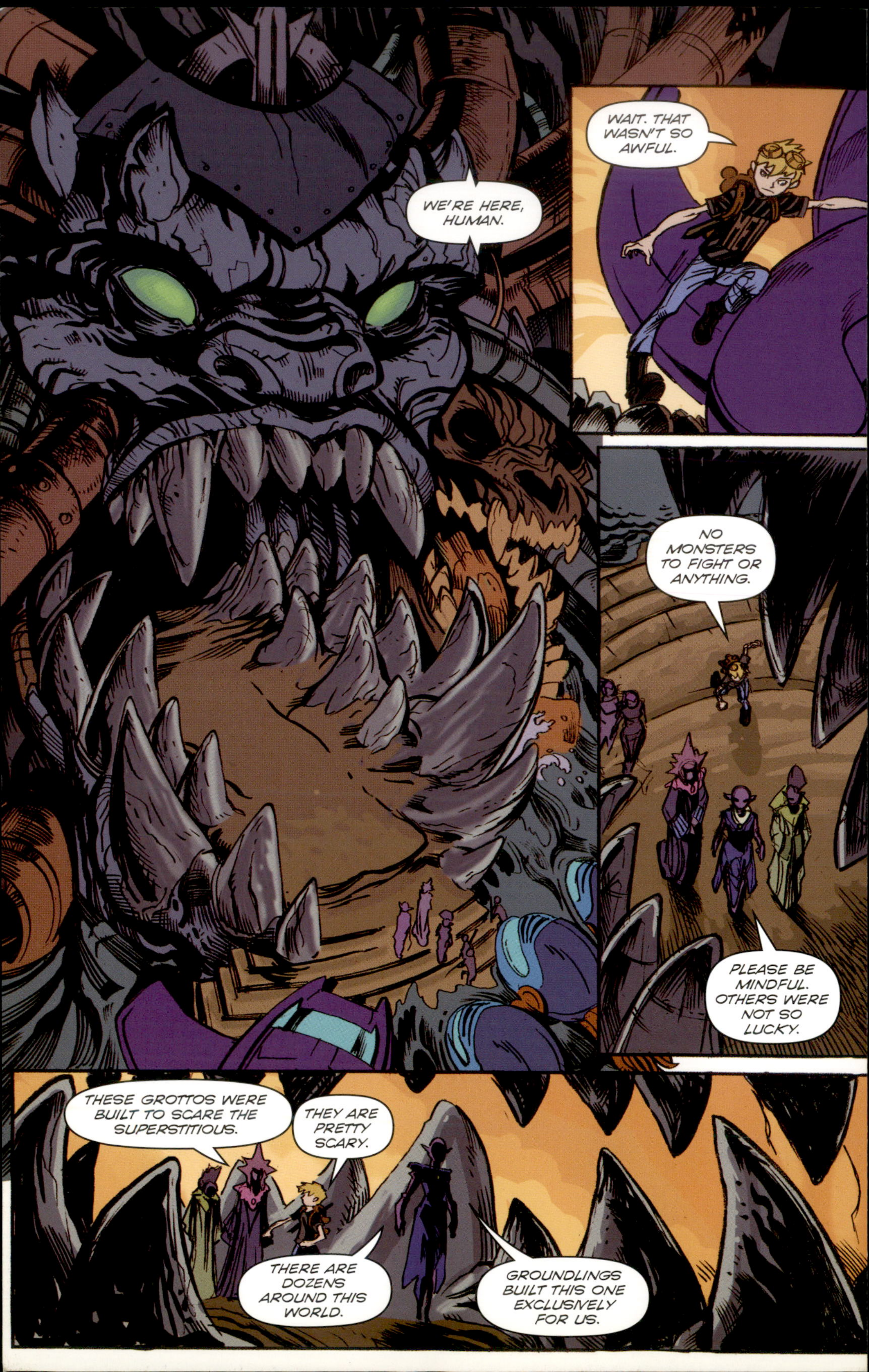
WE'RE HERE, HUMAN.
WAIT. THAT WASN'T SO AWFUL.
NO MONSTERS TO FIGHT OR ANYTHING.
PLEASE BE MINDFUL. OTHERS WERE NOT SO LUCKY.
THESE GROTTOS WERE BUILT TO SCARE THE SUPERSTITIOUS.
THEY ARE PRETTY SCARY.
THERE ARE DOZENS AROUND THIS WORLD.
GROUNDLINGS BUILT THIS ONE EXCLUSIVELY FOR US.

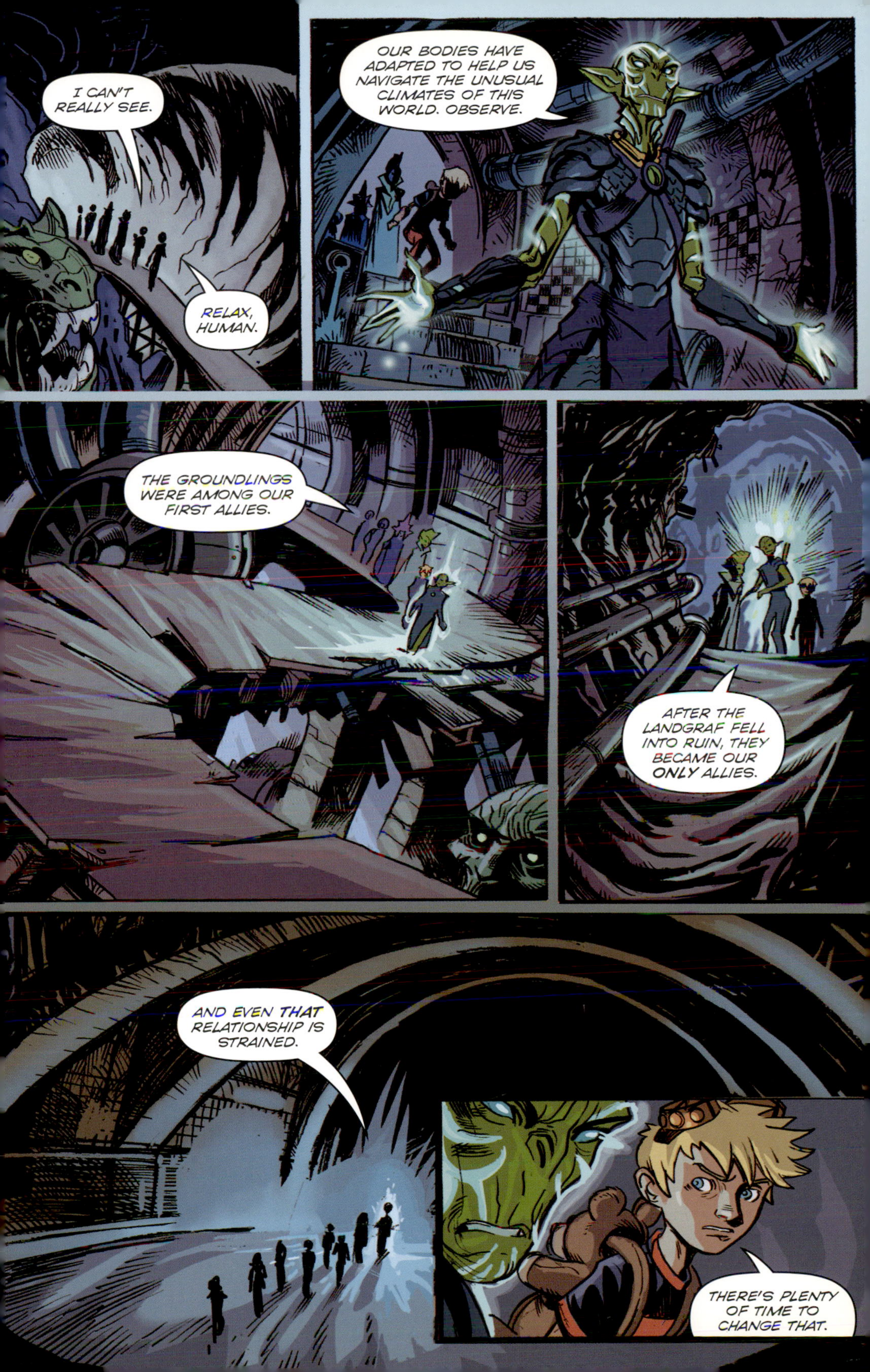
I CAN'T REALLY SEE.
RELAX, HUMAN.
OUR BODIES HAVE ADAPTED TO HELP US NAVIGATE THE UNUSUAL CLIMATES OF THIS WORLD. OBSERVE.
THE GROUNDLINGS WERE AMONG OUR FIRST ALLIES.
AFTER THE LANDGRAF FELL INTO RUIN, THEY BECAME OUR ONLY ALLIES.
AND EVEN THAT RELATIONSHIP IS STRAINED.
THERE'S PLENTY OF TIME TO CHANGE THAT.

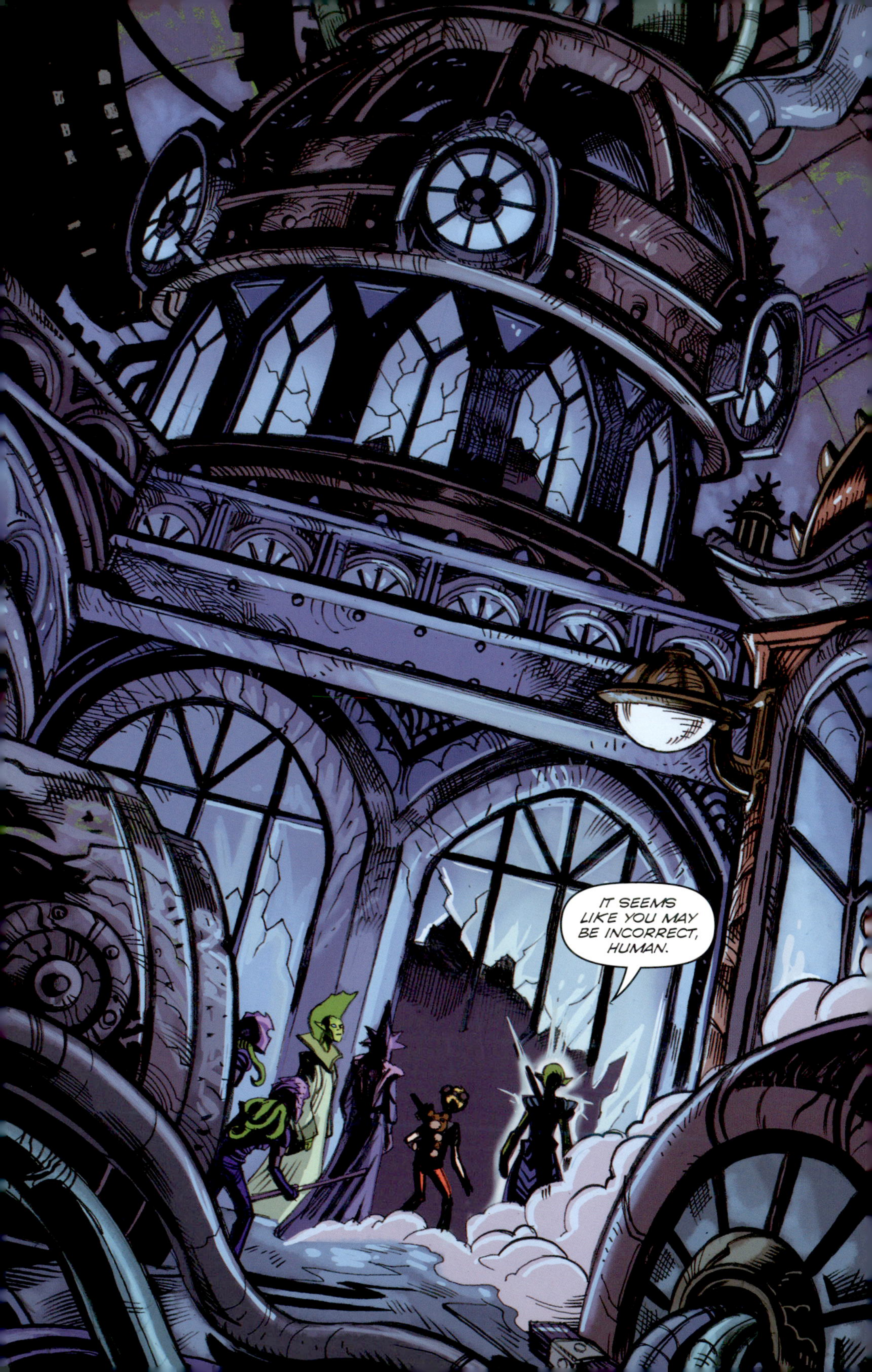
IT SEEMS LIKE YOU MAY BE INCORRECT, HUMAN.

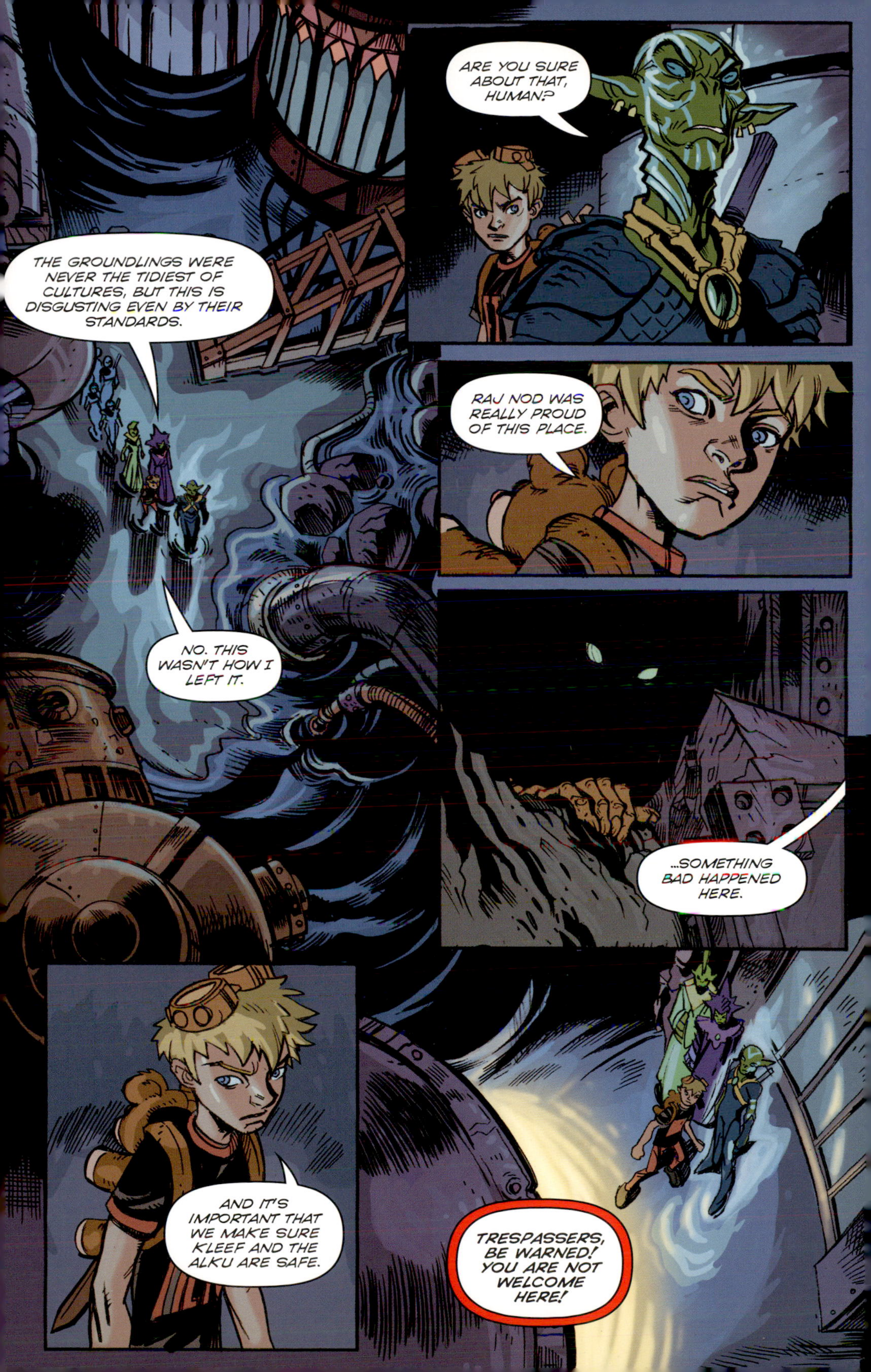
THE GROUNDLINGS WERE NEVER THE TIDIEST OF CULTURES, BUT THIS IS DISGUSTING EVEN BY THEIR STANDARDS.
ARE YOU SURE ABOUT THAT, HUMAN?
RAJ NOD WAS REALLY PROUD OF THIS PLACE.
NO. THIS WASN'T HOW I LEFT IT.
...SOMETHING BAD HAPPENED HERE.
AND IT'S IMPORTANT THAT WE MAKE SURE KLEEF AND THE ALKU ARE SAFE.
TRESPASSERS, BE WARNED! YOU ARE NOT WELCOME HERE!

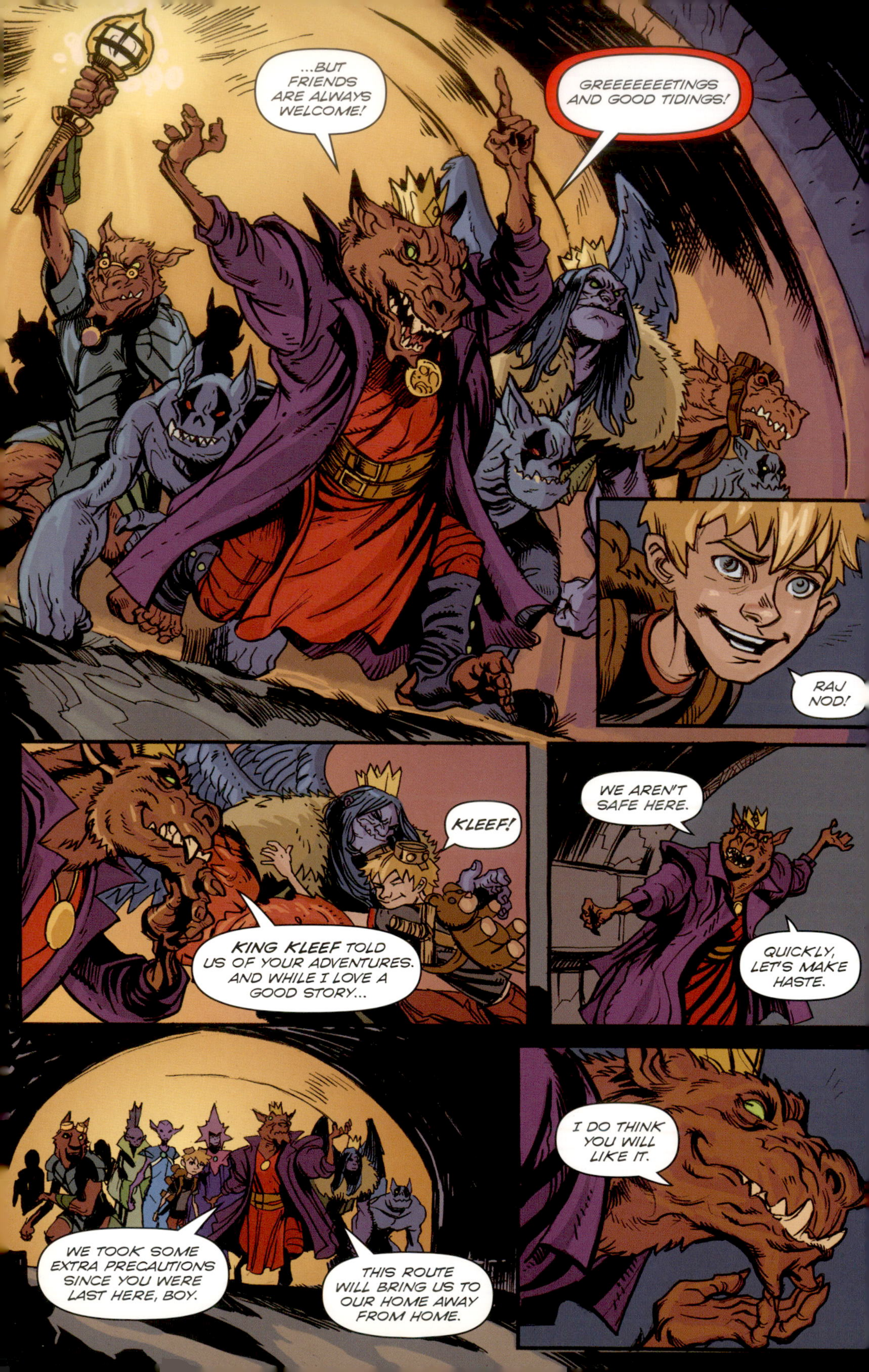
...BUT FRIENDS ARE ALWAYS WELCOME!
GREEEEEEEETINGS AND GOOD TIDINGS!
RAJ NOD!
KLEEF!
KING KLEEF TOLD US OF YOUR ADVENTURES. AND WHILE I LOVE A GOOD STORY...
WE AREN'T SAFE HERE.
QUICKLY, LET'S MAKE HASTE.
WE TOOK SOME EXTRA PRECAUTIONS SINCE YOU WERE LAST HERE, BOY.
THIS ROUTE WILL BRING US TO OUR HOME AWAY FROM HOME.
I DO THINK YOU WILL LIKE IT.

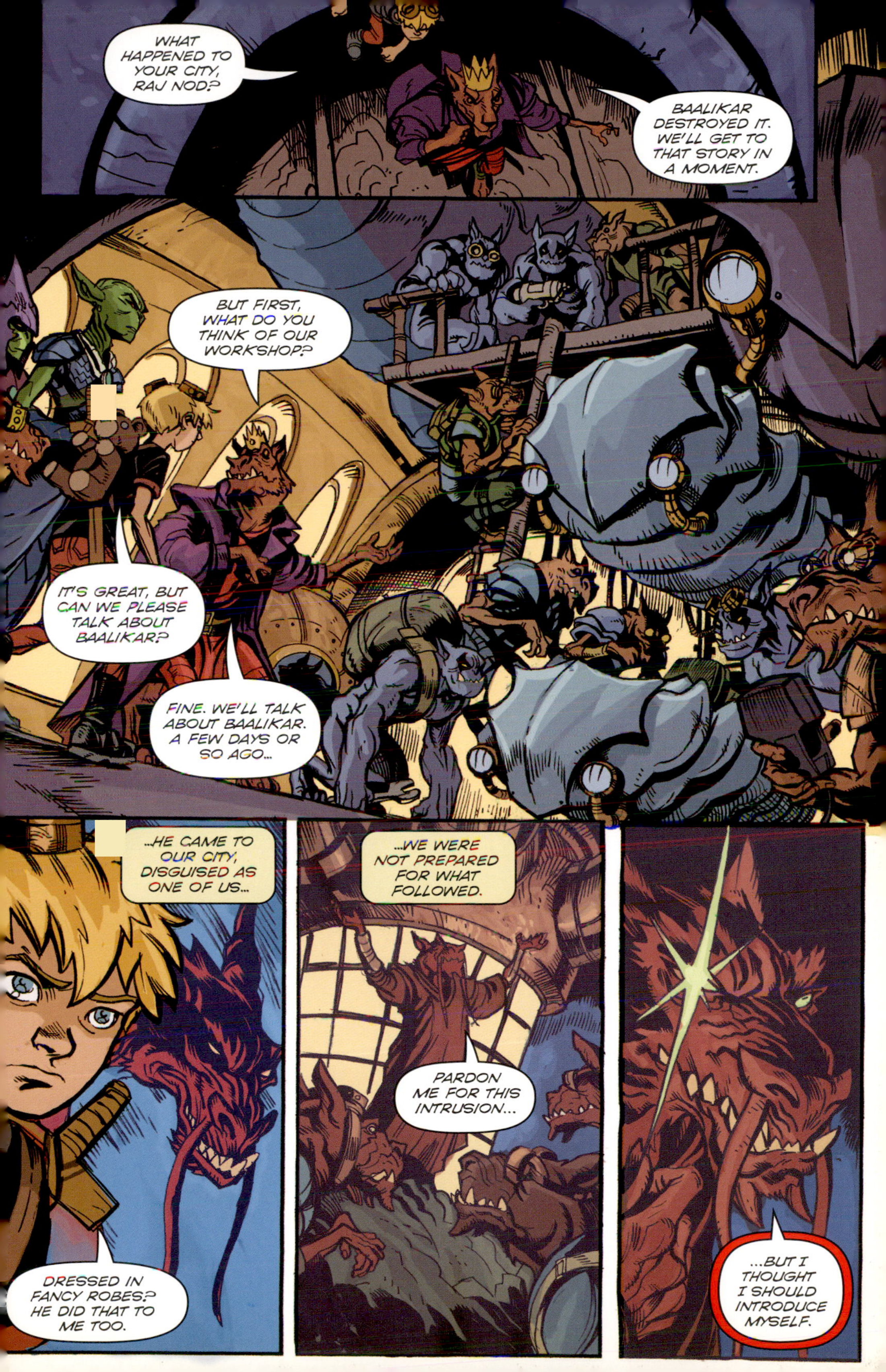
WHAT HAPPENED TO YOUR CITY, RAJ NOD?
BAALIKAR DESTROYED IT. WE'LL GET TO THAT STORY IN A MOMENT.
BUT FIRST, WHAT DO YOU THINK OF OUR WORKSHOP?
IT'S GREAT, BUT CAN WE PLEASE TALK ABOUT BAALIKAR?
FINE. WE'LL TALK ABOUT BAALIKAR. A FEW DAYS OR SO AGO...
...HE CAME TO OUR CITY, DISGUISED AS ONE OF US...
DRESSED IN FANCY ROBES? HE DID THAT TO ME TOO.
...WE WERE NOT PREPARED FOR WHAT FOLLOWED.
PARDON ME FOR THIS INTRUSION...
...BUT I THOUGHT I SHOULD INTRODUCE MYSELF.

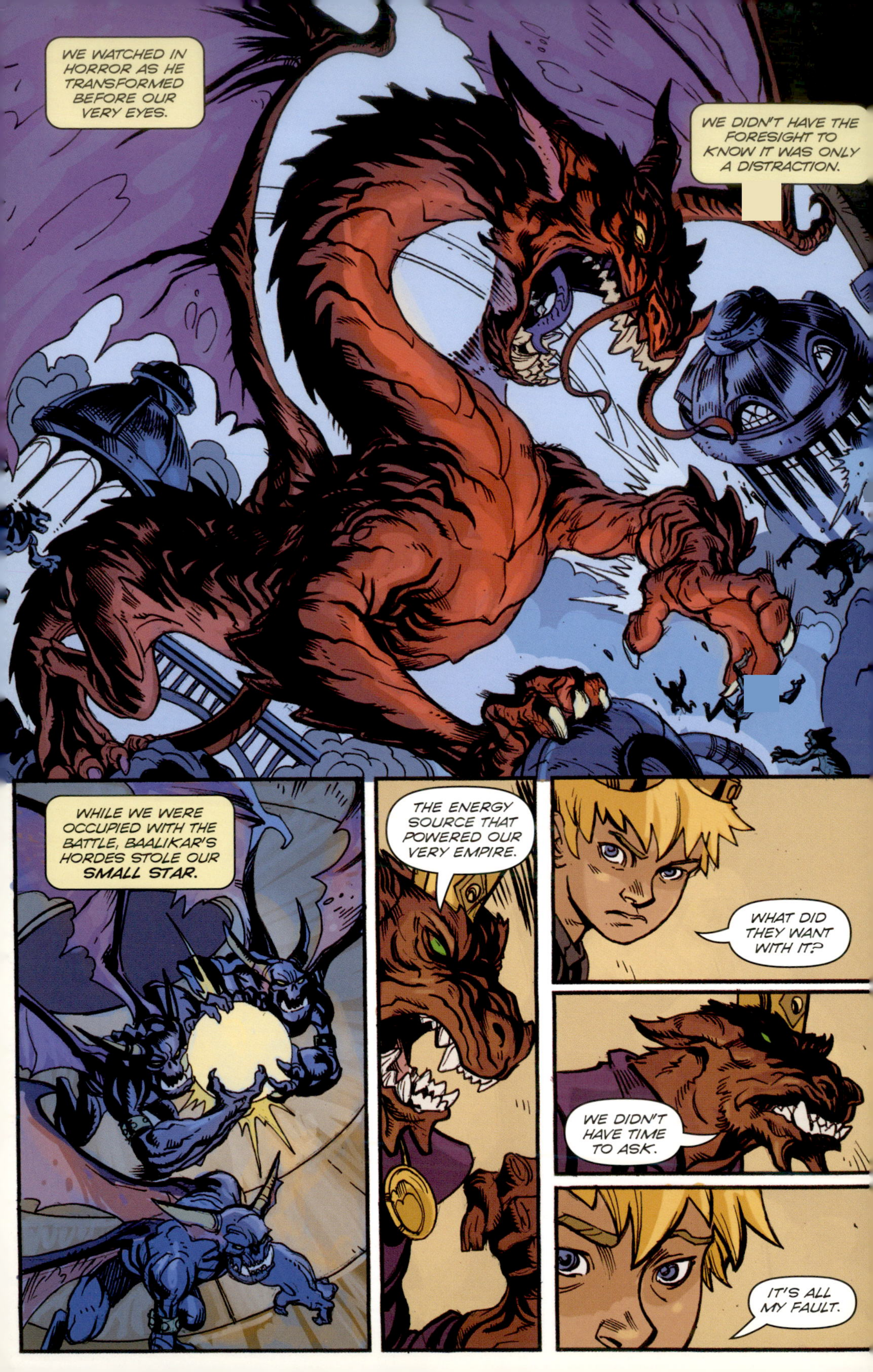
WE WATCHED IN HORROR AS HE TRANSFORMED BEFORE OUR VERY EYES.
WE DIDN'T HAVE THE FORESIGHT TO KNOW IT WAS ONLY A DISTRACTION.
WHILE WE WERE OCCUPIED WITH THE BATTLE, BAALIKAR'S HORDES STOLE OUR **SMALL STAR.**
THE ENERGY SOURCE THAT POWERED OUR VERY EMPIRE.
WHAT DID THEY WANT WITH IT?
WE DIDN'T HAVE TIME TO ASK.
IT'S ALL MY FAULT.

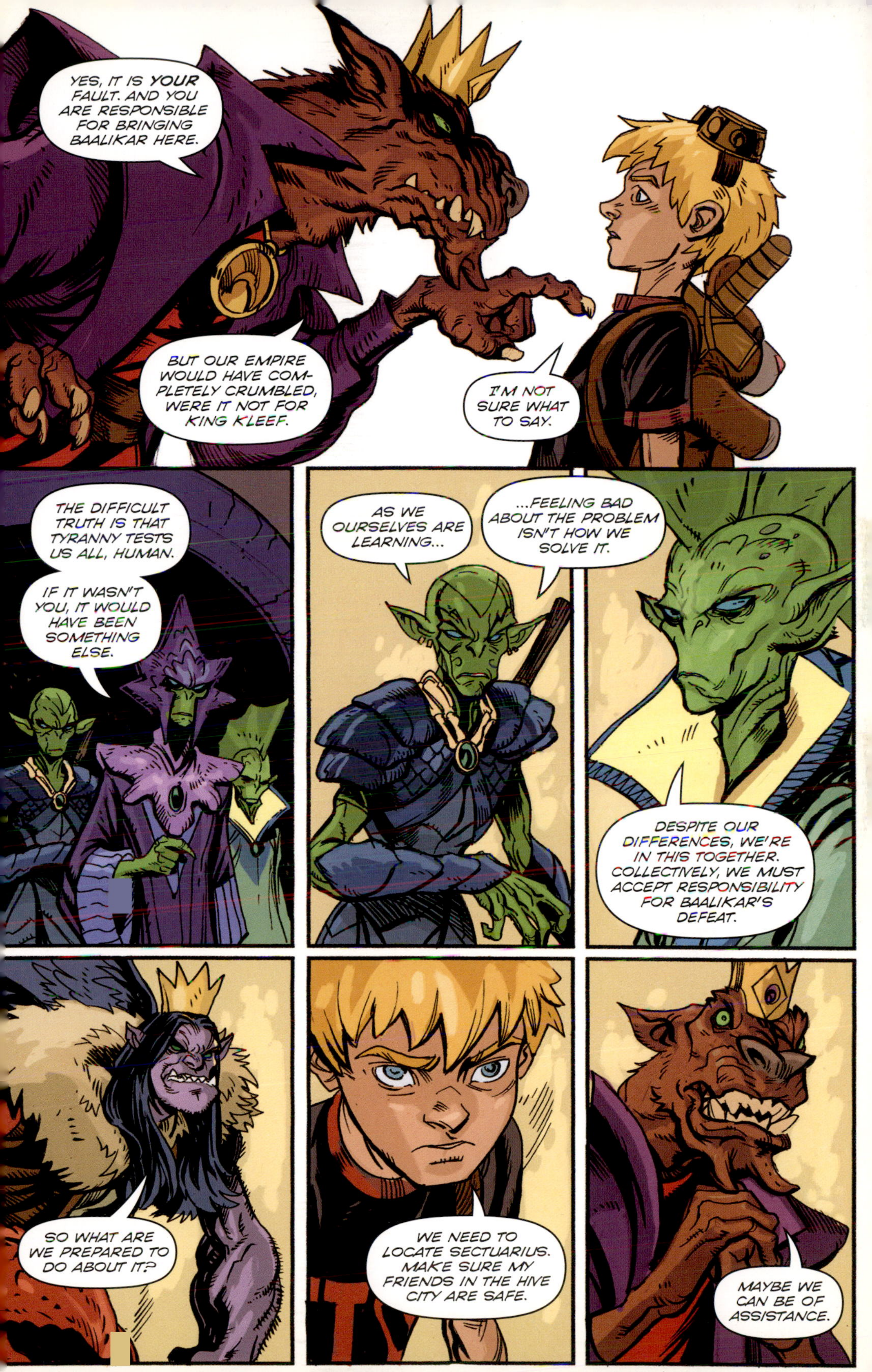
YES, IT IS YOUR FAULT. AND YOU ARE RESPONSIBLE FOR BRINGING BAALIKAR HERE.
BUT OUR EMPIRE WOULD HAVE COMPLETELY CRUMBLED, WERE IT NOT FOR KING KLEEF.
I'M NOT SURE WHAT TO SAY.
THE DIFFICULT TRUTH IS THAT TYRANNY TESTS US ALL, HUMAN.
IF IT WASN'T YOU, IT WOULD HAVE BEEN SOMETHING ELSE.
AS WE OURSELVES ARE LEARNING...
...FEELING BAD ABOUT THE PROBLEM ISN'T HOW WE SOLVE IT.
DESPITE OUR DIFFERENCES, WE'RE IN THIS TOGETHER. COLLECTIVELY, WE MUST ACCEPT RESPONSIBILITY FOR BAALIKAR'S DEFEAT.
SO WHAT ARE WE PREPARED TO DO ABOUT IT?
WE NEED TO LOCATE SECTUARIUS. MAKE SURE MY FRIENDS IN THE HIVE CITY ARE SAFE.
MAYBE WE CAN BE OF ASSISTANCE.

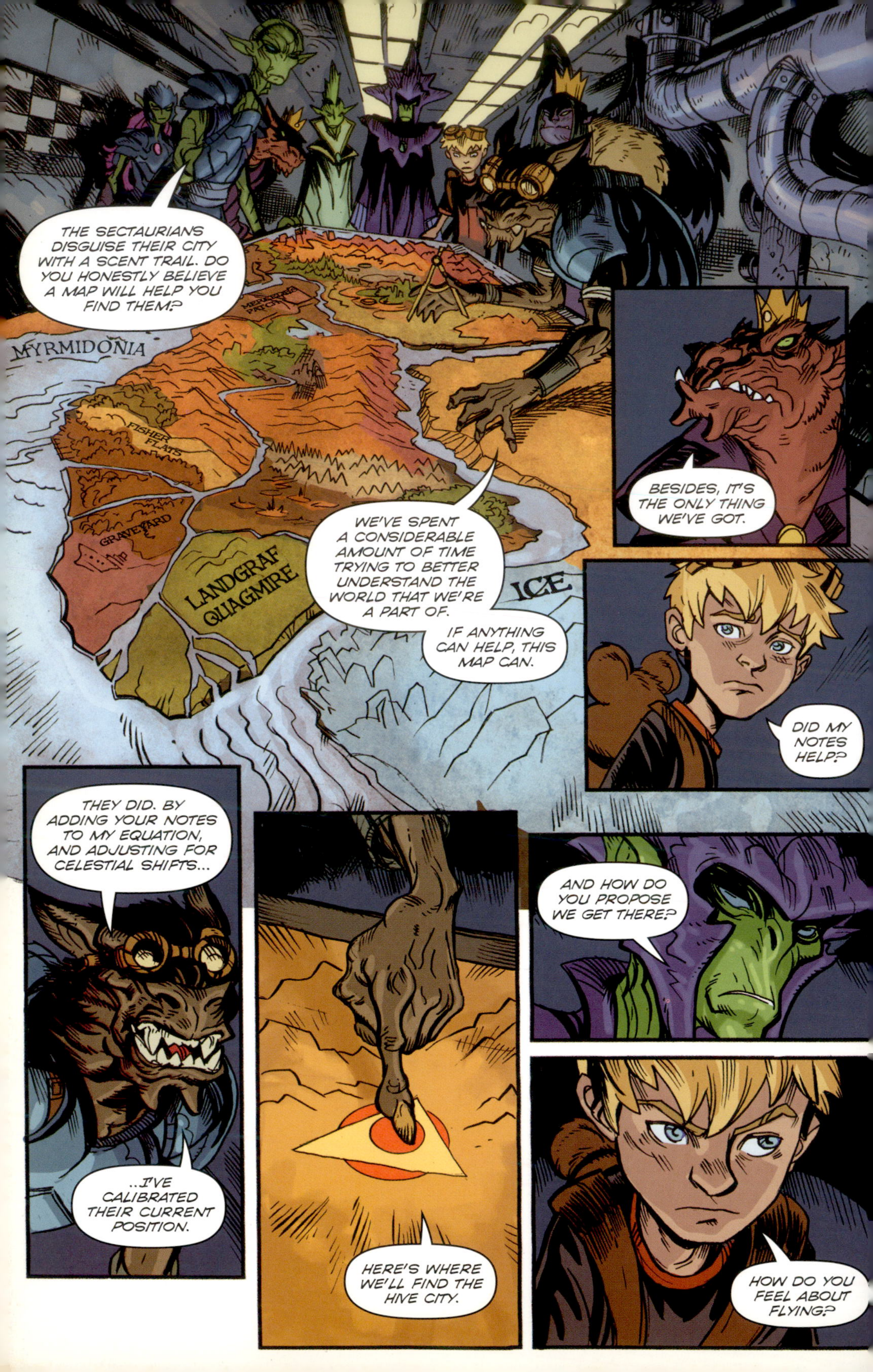
THE SECTAURIANS DISGUISE THEIR CITY WITH A SCENT TRAIL. DO YOU HONESTLY BELIEVE A MAP WILL HELP YOU FIND THEM?
MYRMIDONIA
FISHER FLATS
GRAVEYARD
LANDGRAF QUAGMIRE
ICE
WE'VE SPENT A CONSIDERABLE AMOUNT OF TIME TRYING TO BETTER UNDERSTAND THE WORLD THAT WE'RE A PART OF.
IF ANYTHING CAN HELP, THIS MAP CAN.
BESIDES, IT'S THE ONLY THING WE'VE GOT.
DID MY NOTES HELP?
THEY DID. BY ADDING YOUR NOTES TO MY EQUATION, AND ADJUSTING FOR CELESTIAL SHIFTS...
...I'VE CALIBRATED THEIR CURRENT POSITION.
HERE'S WHERE WE'LL FIND THE HIVE CITY.
AND HOW DO YOU PROPOSE WE GET THERE?
HOW DO YOU FEEL ABOUT FLYING?

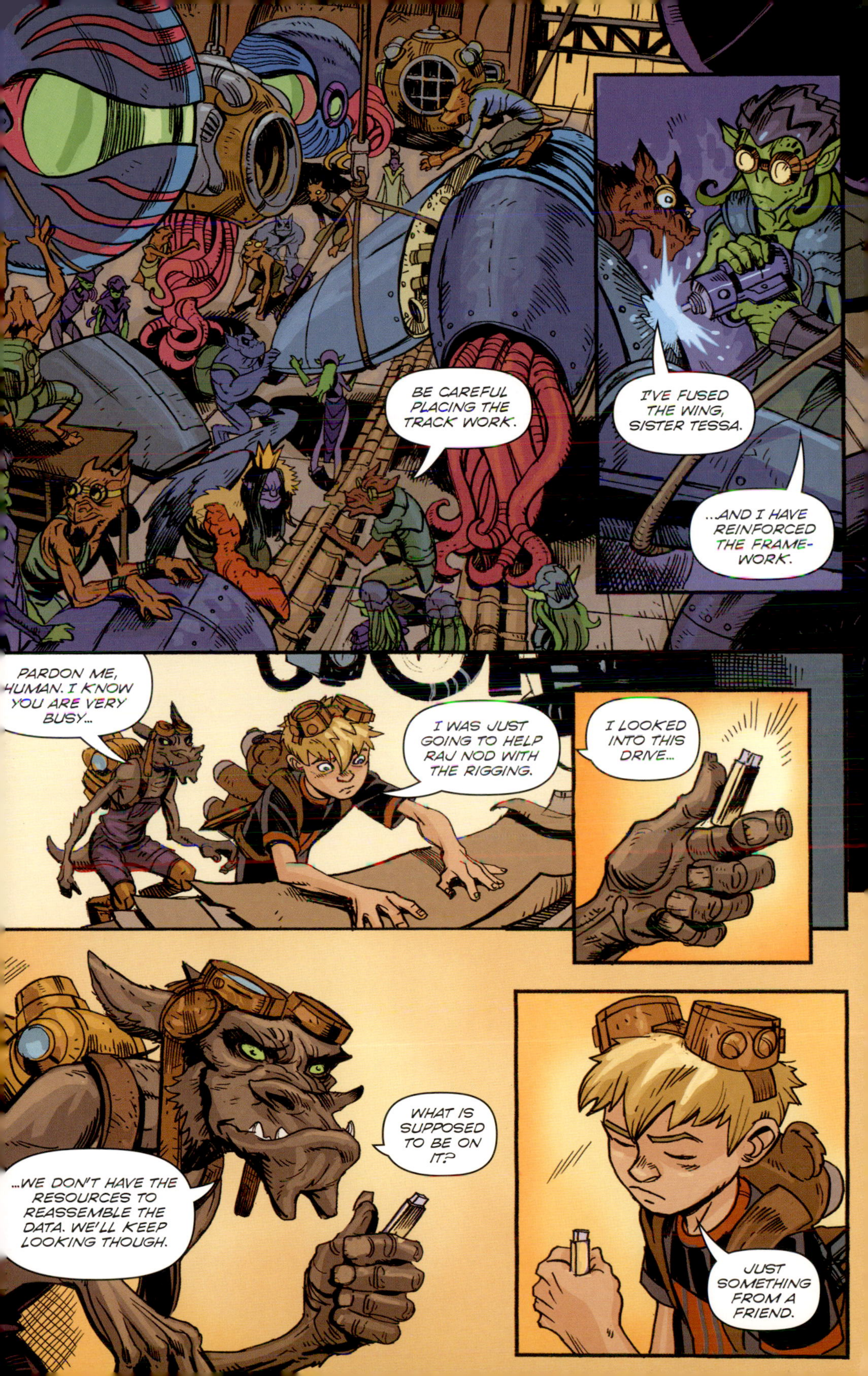
BE CAREFUL PLACING THE TRACK WORK.
I'VE FUSED THE WING, SISTER TESSA.
...AND I HAVE REINFORCED THE FRAME-WORK.
PARDON ME, HUMAN. I KNOW YOU ARE VERY BUSY...
I WAS JUST GOING TO HELP RAJ NOD WITH THE RIGGING.
I LOOKED INTO THIS DRIVE...
WHAT IS SUPPOSED TO BE ON IT?
...WE DON'T HAVE THE RESOURCES TO REASSEMBLE THE DATA. WE'LL KEEP LOOKING THOUGH.
JUST SOMETHING FROM A FRIEND.

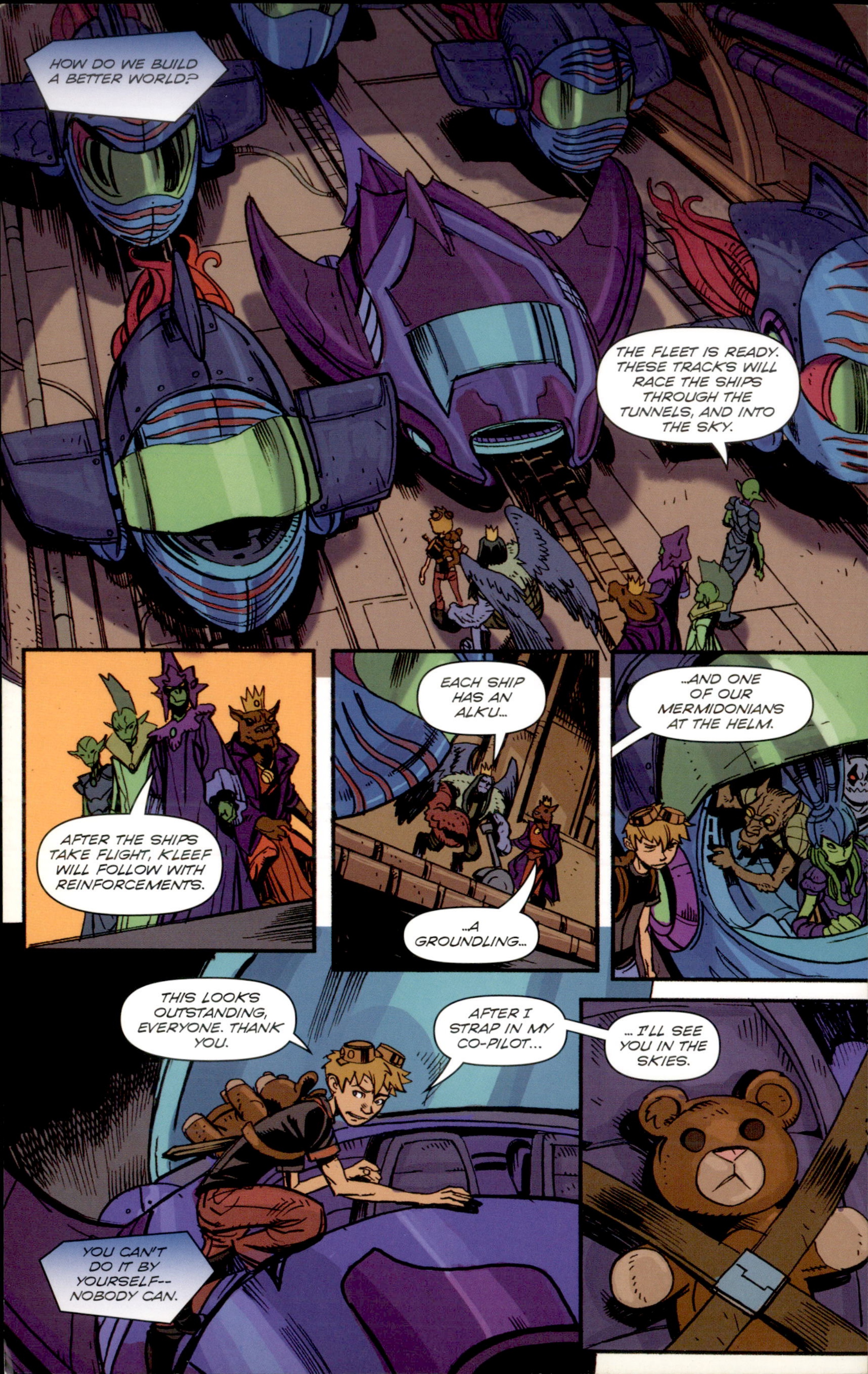
HOW DO WE BUILD A BETTER WORLD?
THE FLEET IS READY. THESE TRACKS WILL RACE THE SHIPS THROUGH THE TUNNELS, AND INTO THE SKY.
AFTER THE SHIPS TAKE FLIGHT, KLEEF WILL FOLLOW WITH REINFORCEMENTS.
EACH SHIP HAS AN ALKU...
...A GROUNDLING...
...AND ONE OF OUR MERMIDONIANS AT THE HELM.
THIS LOOKS OUTSTANDING, EVERYONE. THANK YOU.
AFTER I STRAP IN MY CO-PILOT...
... I'LL SEE YOU IN THE SKIES.
YOU CAN'T DO IT BY YOURSELF-- NOBODY CAN.

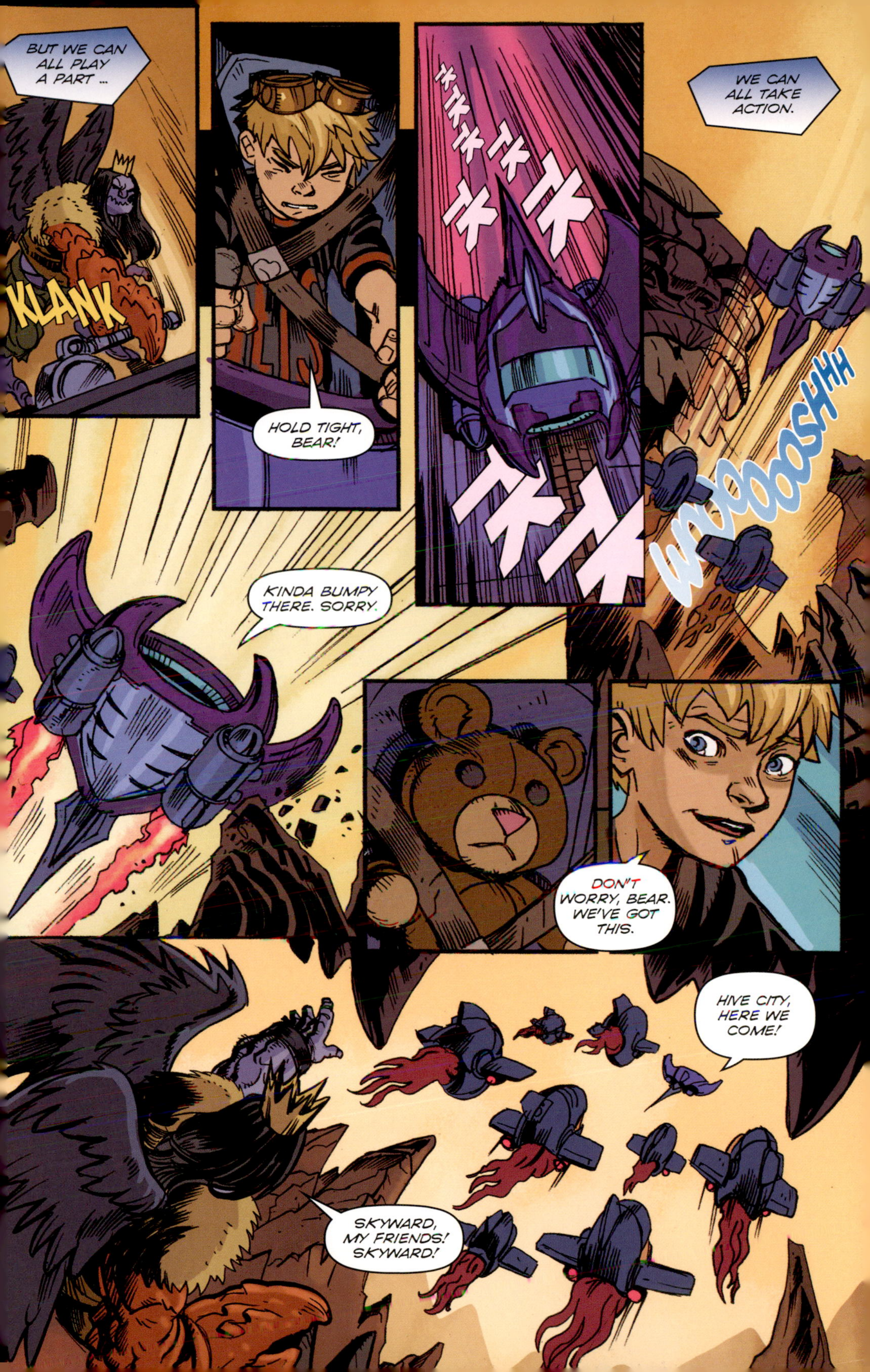

BUT WE CAN ALL PLAY A PART ...
KLANK
HOLD TIGHT, BEAR!
TK TK TK TK TK TK
TK TK TK
WE CAN ALL TAKE ACTION.
WOOOOOSHHH
KINDA BUMPY THERE. SORRY.
DON'T WORRY, BEAR. WE'VE GOT THIS.
HIVE CITY, HERE WE COME!
SKYWARD, MY FRIENDS! SKYWARD!

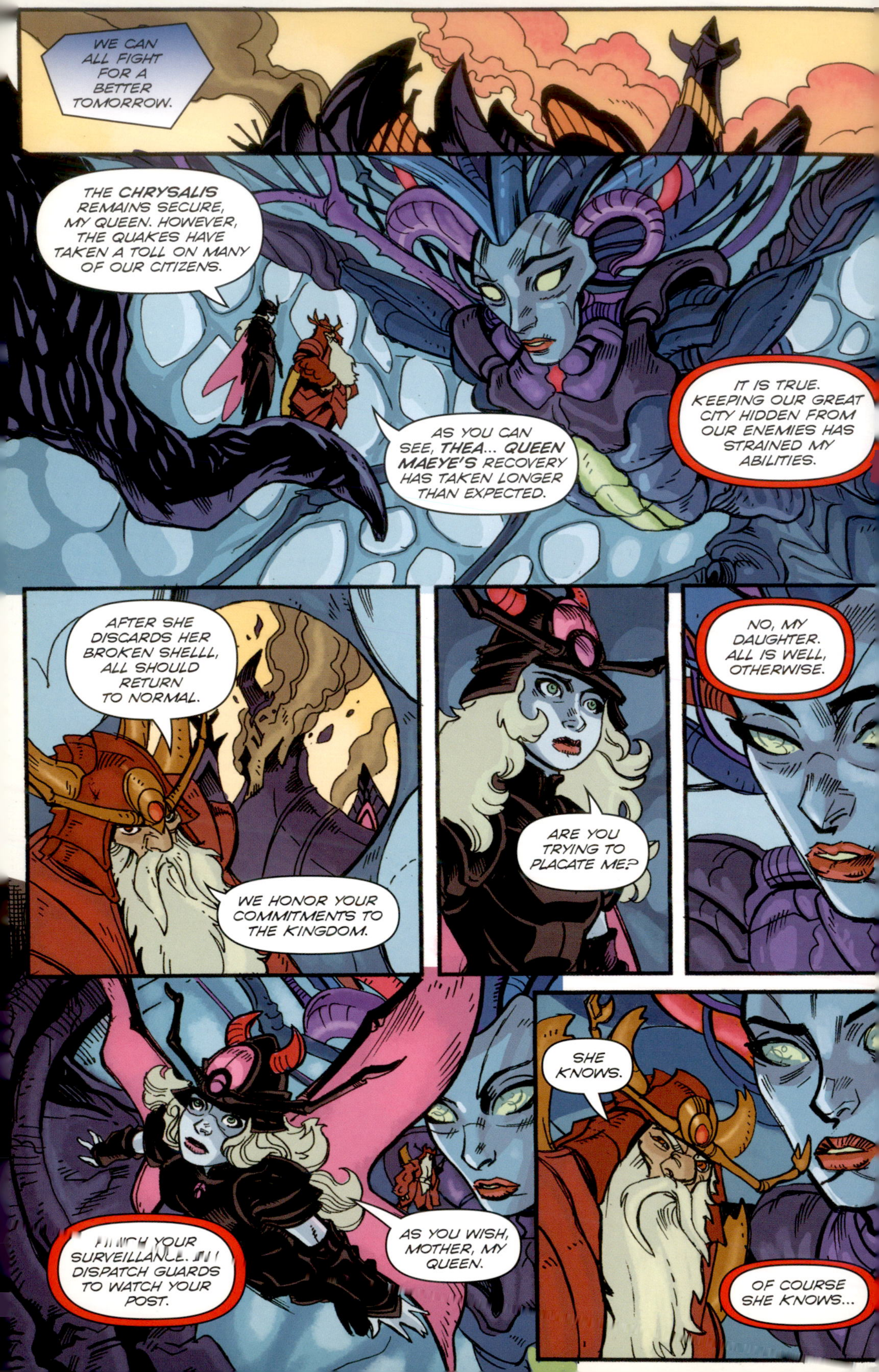
WE CAN ALL FIGHT FOR A BETTER TOMORROW.
THE CHRYSALIS REMAINS SECURE, MY QUEEN. HOWEVER, THE QUAKES HAVE TAKEN A TOLL ON MANY OF OUR CITIZENS.
AS YOU CAN SEE, THEA... QUEEN MAEYE'S RECOVERY HAS TAKEN LONGER THAN EXPECTED.
IT IS TRUE. KEEPING OUR GREAT CITY HIDDEN FROM OUR ENEMIES HAS STRAINED MY ABILITIES.
AFTER SHE DISCARDS HER BROKEN SHELLL, ALL SHOULD RETURN TO NORMAL.
WE HONOR YOUR COMMITMENTS TO THE KINGDOM.
ARE YOU TRYING TO PLACATE ME?
NO, MY DAUGHTER. ALL IS WELL, OTHERWISE.
YOUR SURVEILLANC
DISPATCH GUARDS TO WATCH YOUR POST.
AS YOU WISH, MOTHER, MY QUEEN.
SHE KNOWS.
OF COURSE SHE KNOWS...

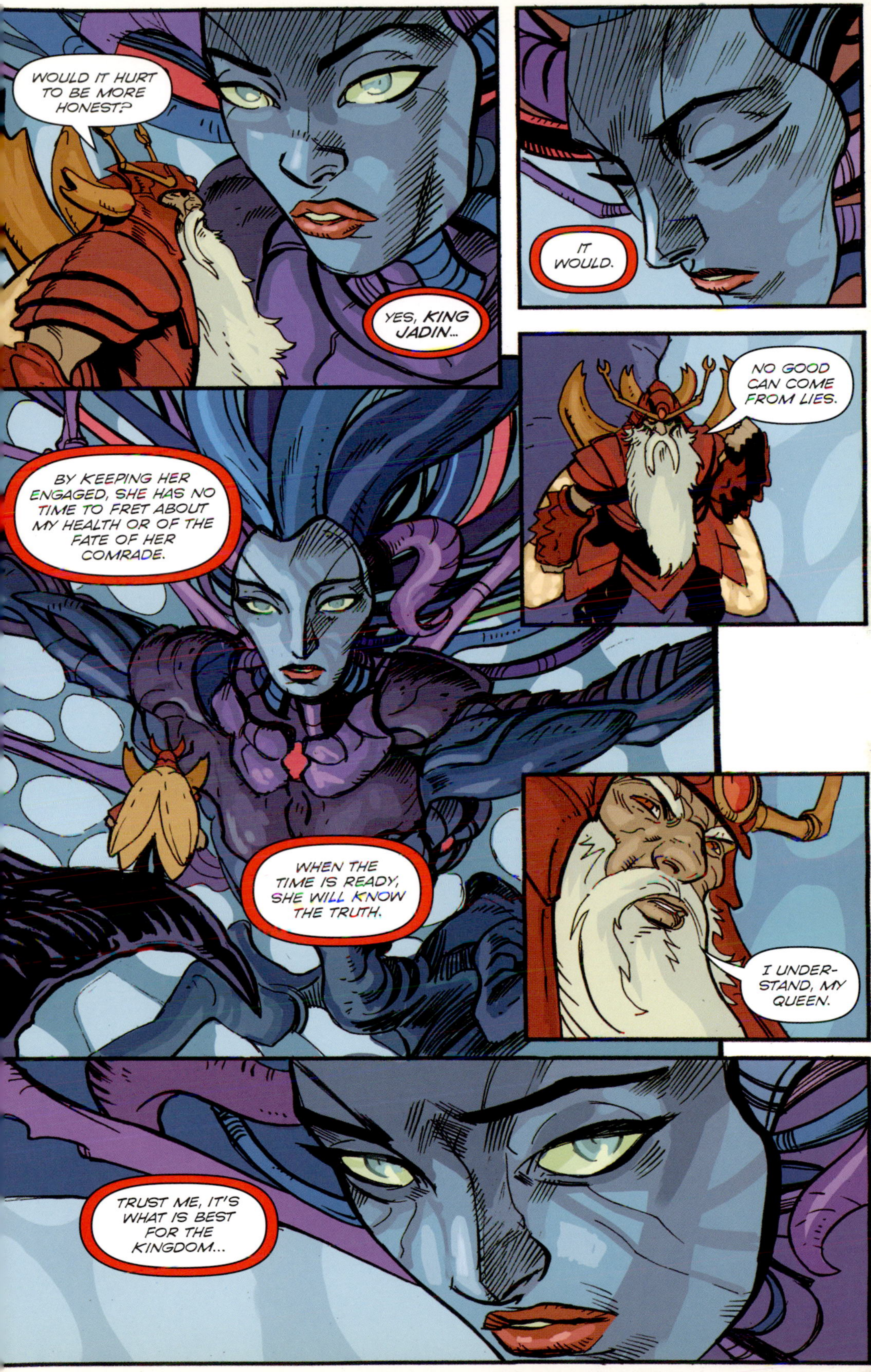
WOULD IT HURT TO BE MORE HONEST?
YES, KING JADIN...
IT WOULD.
NO GOOD CAN COME FROM LIES.
BY KEEPING HER ENGAGED, SHE HAS NO TIME TO FRET ABOUT MY HEALTH OR OF THE FATE OF HER COMRADE.
WHEN THE TIME IS READY, SHE WILL KNOW THE TRUTH.
I UNDER-STAND, MY QUEEN.
TRUST ME, IT'S WHAT IS BEST FOR THE KINGDOM...

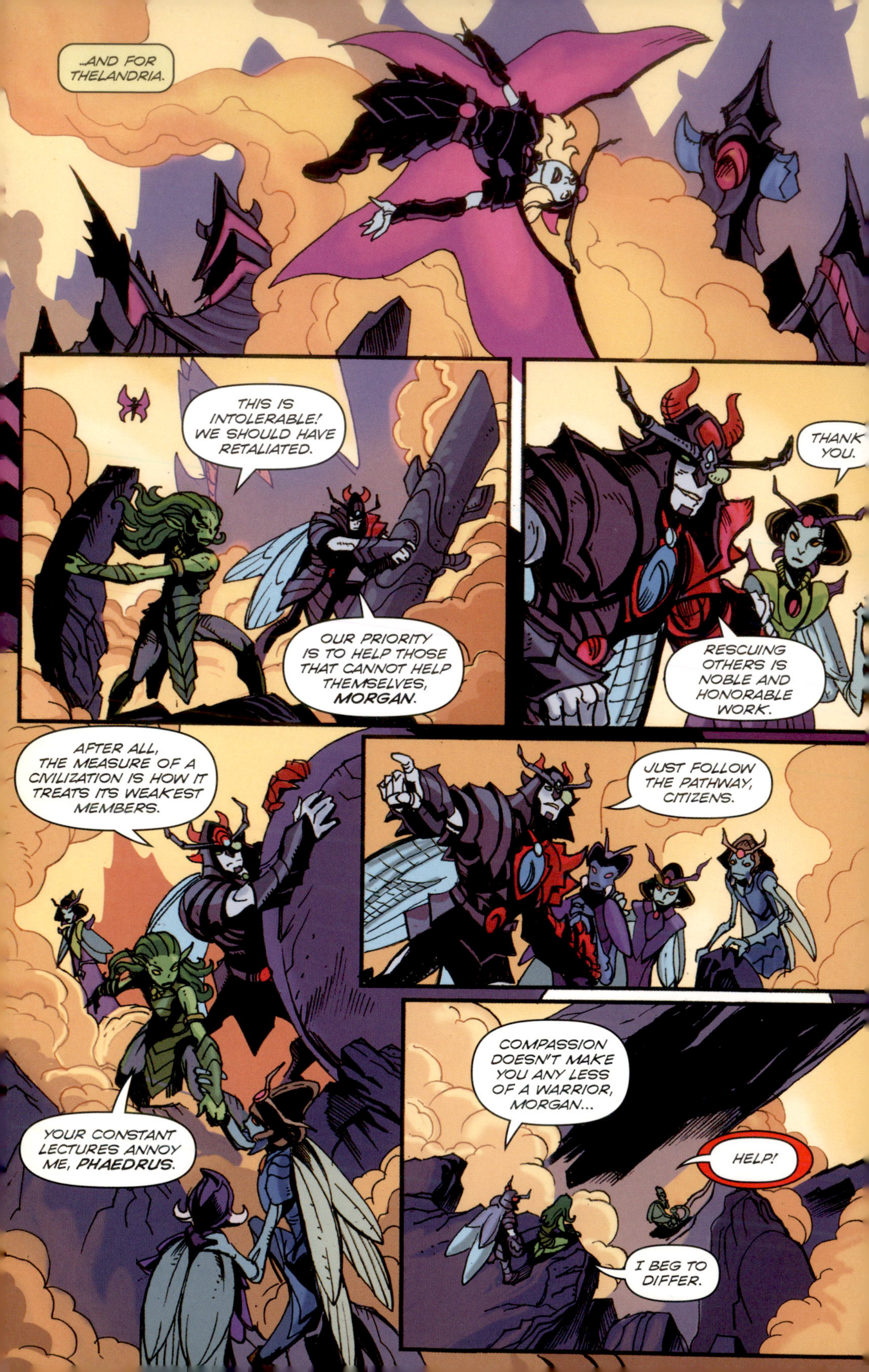

...AND FOR THELANDRIA.
THIS IS INTOLERABLE! WE SHOULD HAVE RETALIATED.
OUR PRIORITY IS TO HELP THOSE THAT CANNOT HELP THEMSELVES, MORGAN.
THANK YOU.
RESCUING OTHERS IS NOBLE AND HONORABLE WORK.
AFTER ALL, THE MEASURE OF A CIVILIZATION IS HOW IT TREATS ITS WEAKEST MEMBERS.
YOUR CONSTANT LECTURES ANNOY ME, PHAEDRUS.
JUST FOLLOW THE PATHWAY, CITIZENS.
COMPASSION DOESN'T MAKE YOU ANY LESS OF A WARRIOR, MORGAN...
HELP!
I BEG TO DIFFER.

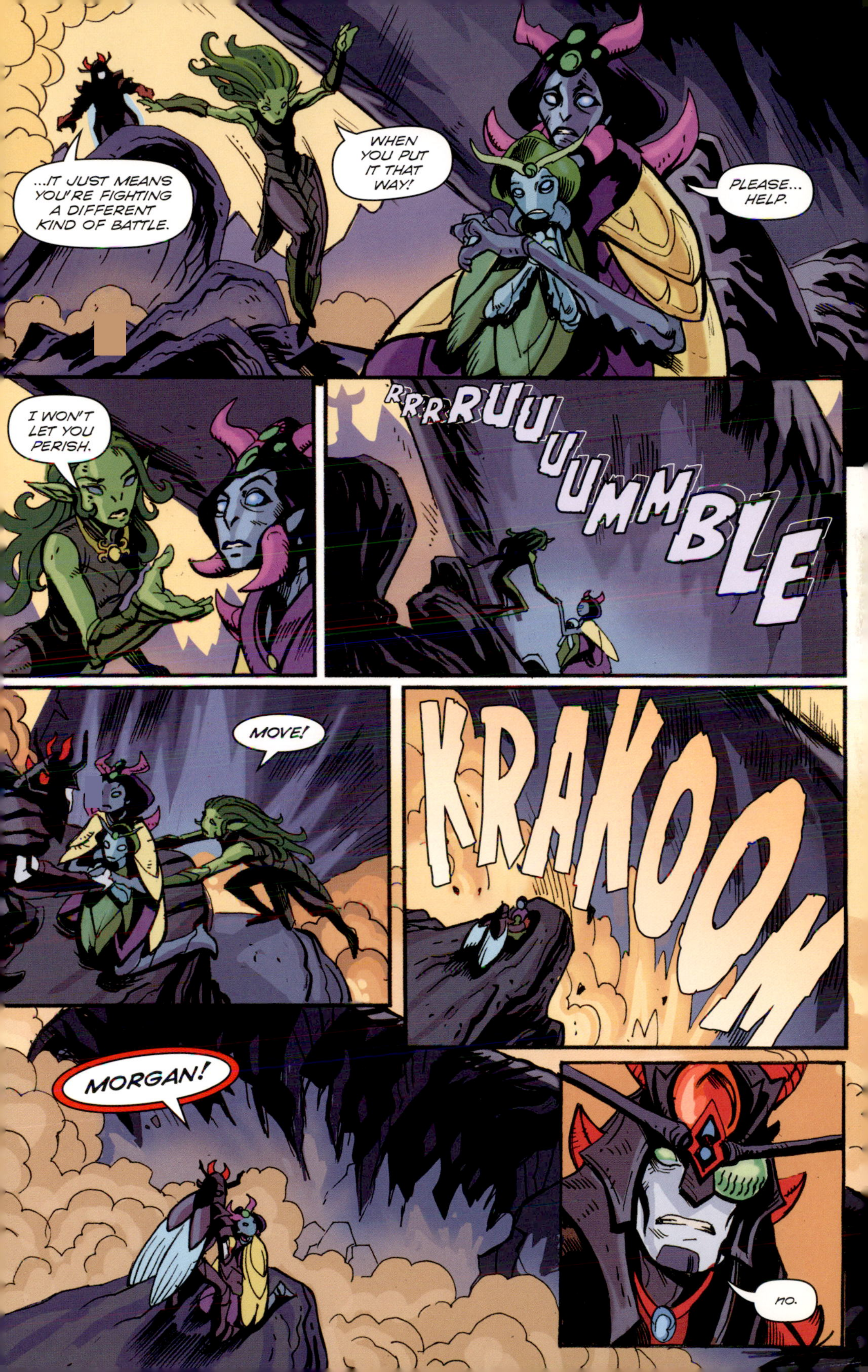

...IT JUST MEANS YOU'RE FIGHTING A DIFFERENT KIND OF BATTLE.
WHEN YOU PUT IT THAT WAY!
PLEASE... HELP.
I WON'T LET YOU PERISH.
RRRRUUUUMMBLE
MOVE!
KRAKOOM
MORGAN!
no.

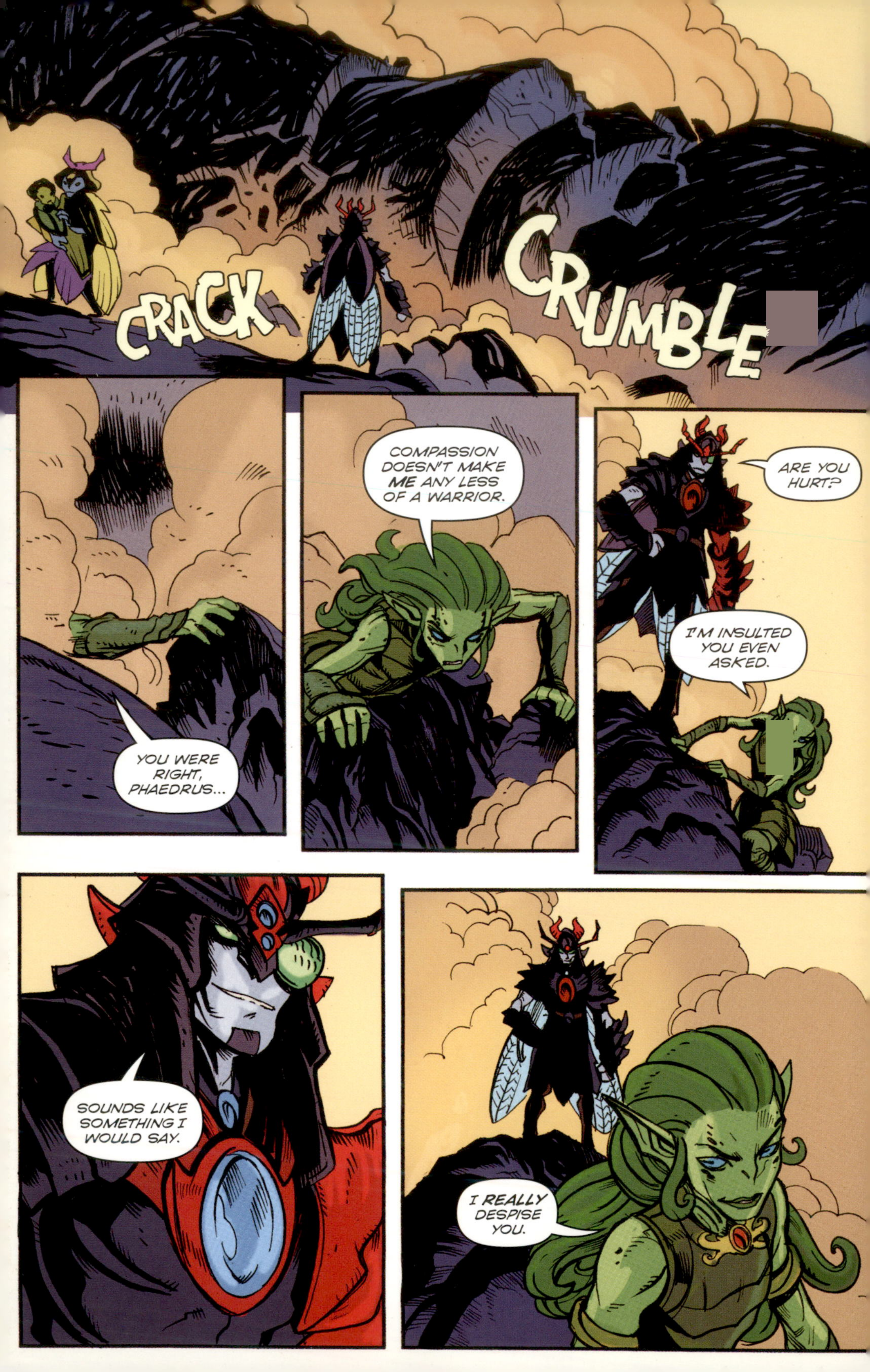
CRACK
CRUMBLE
YOU WERE RIGHT, PHAEDRUS...
COMPASSION DOESN'T MAKE ME ANY LESS OF A WARRIOR.
ARE YOU HURT?
I'M INSULTED YOU EVEN ASKED.
SOUNDS LIKE SOMETHING I WOULD SAY.
I REALLY DESPISE YOU.

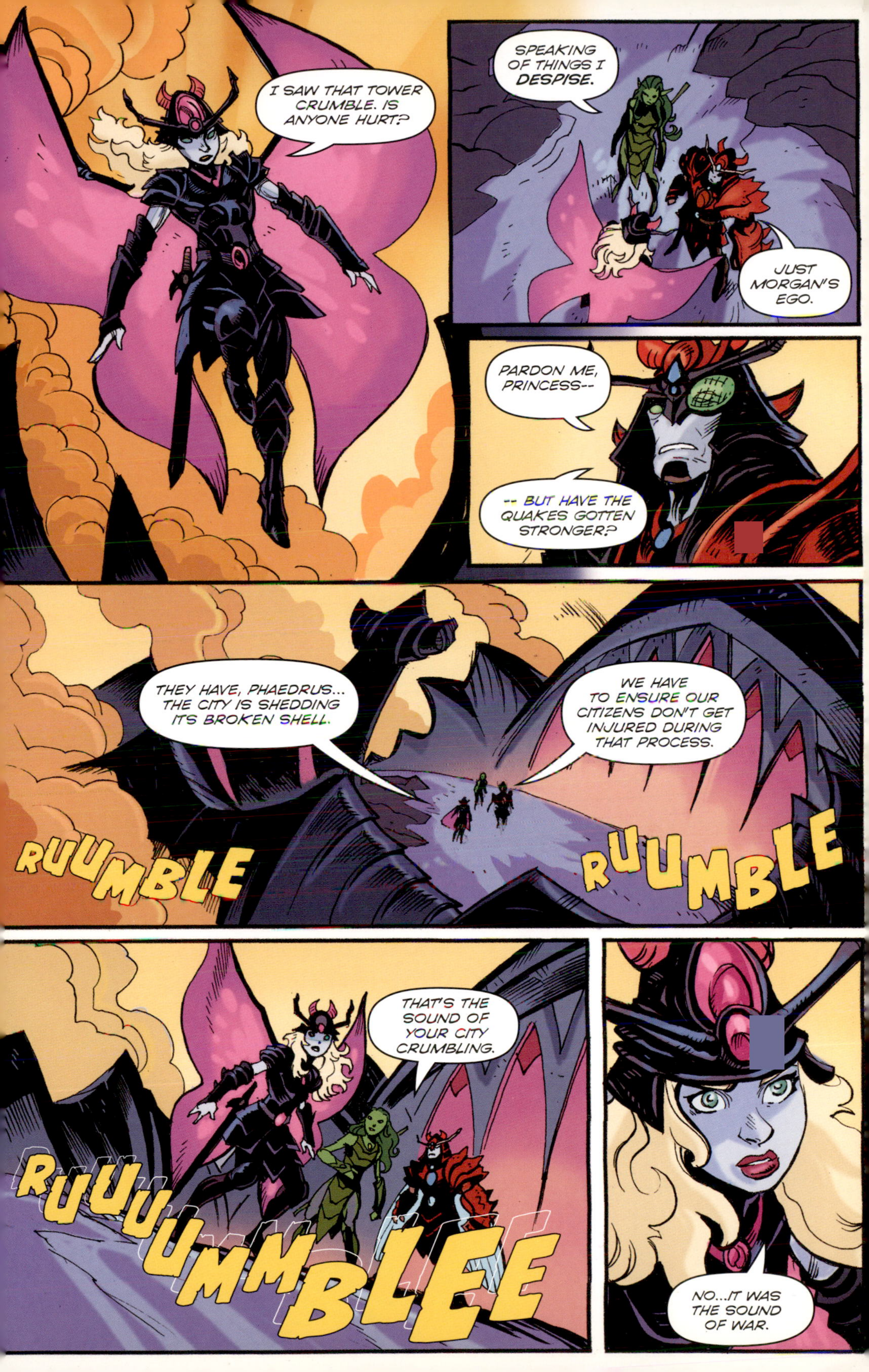
I SAW THAT TOWER CRUMBLE. IS ANYONE HURT?
SPEAKING OF THINGS I DESPISE.
JUST MORGAN'S EGO.
PARDON ME, PRINCESS--
-- BUT HAVE THE QUAKES GOTTEN STRONGER?
THEY HAVE, PHAEDRUS... THE CITY IS SHEDDING ITS BROKEN SHELL.
WE HAVE TO ENSURE OUR CITIZENS DON'T GET INJURED DURING THAT PROCESS.
RUUMBLE
RUUMBLE
THAT'S THE SOUND OF YOUR CITY CRUMBLING.
RUUUUMMBLEE
NO...IT WAS THE SOUND OF WAR.

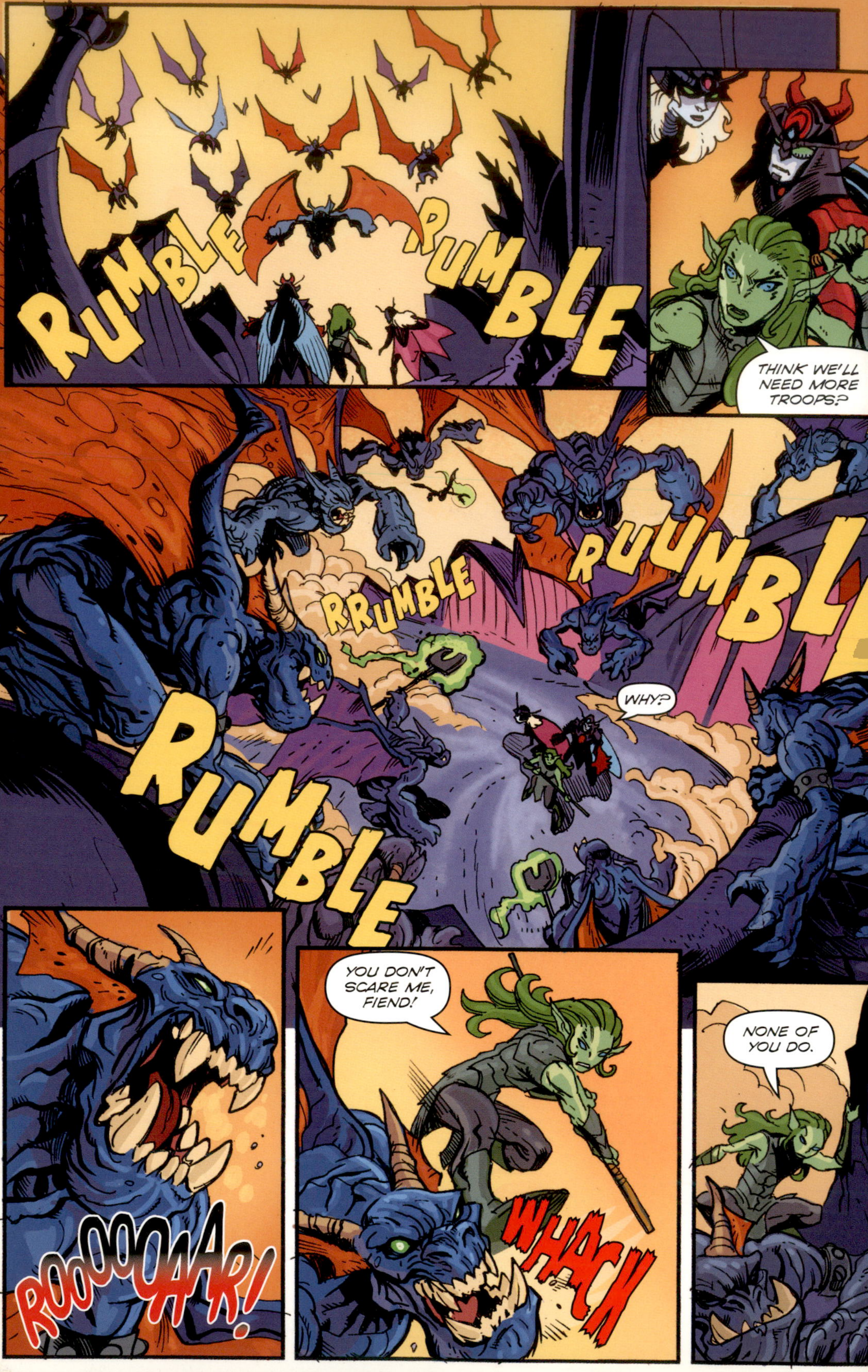
RUMBLE RUMBLE
THINK WE'LL NEED MORE TROOPS?
RRUMBLE
RUUMBLE
RUMBLE
WHY?
ROOOOOAR!
YOU DON'T SCARE ME, FIEND!
WHACK
NONE OF YOU DO.

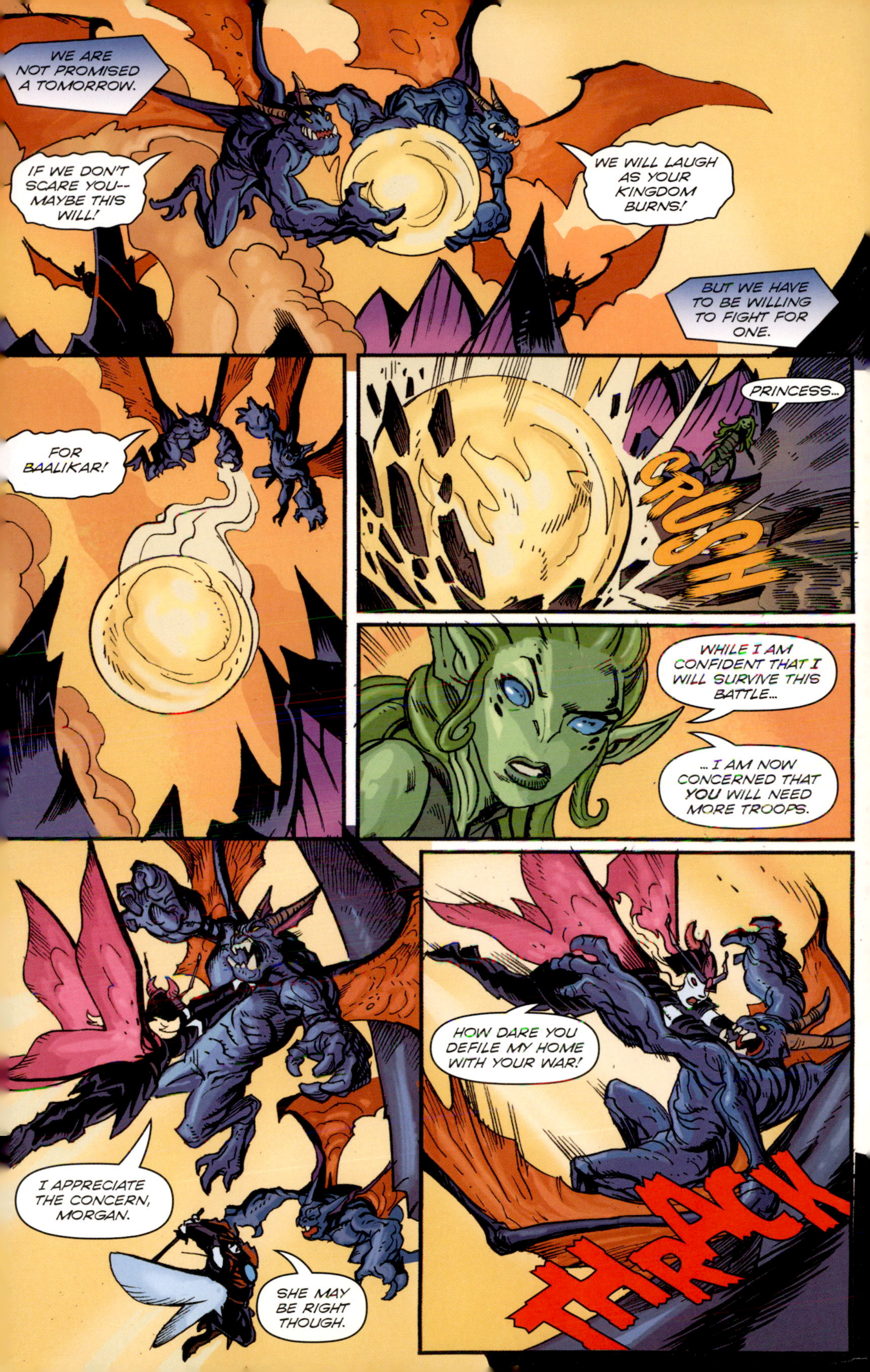
WE ARE NOT PROMISED A TOMORROW.
IF WE DON'T SCARE YOU-- MAYBE THIS WILL!
WE WILL LAUGH AS YOUR KINGDOM BURNS!
BUT WE HAVE TO BE WILLING TO FIGHT FOR ONE.
FOR BAALIKAR!
PRINCESS...
CRUSH
WHILE I AM CONFIDENT THAT I WILL SURVIVE THIS BATTLE...
...I AM NOW CONCERNED THAT YOU WILL NEED MORE TROOPS.
I APPRECIATE THE CONCERN, MORGAN.
SHE MAY BE RIGHT THOUGH.
HOW DARE YOU DEFILE MY HOME WITH YOUR WAR!
THRACK

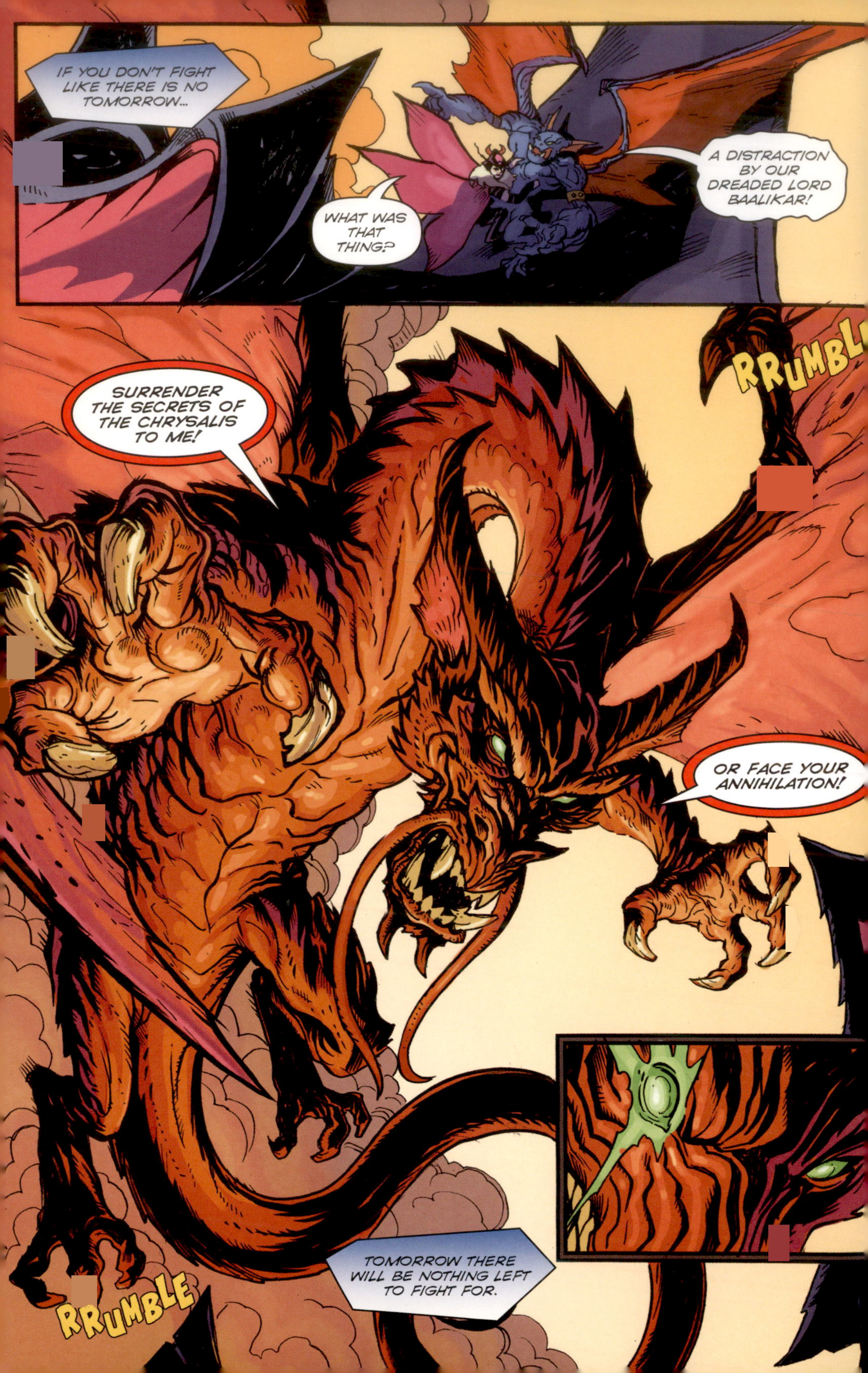
IF YOU DON'T FIGHT LIKE THERE IS NO TOMORROW...
WHAT WAS THAT THING?
A DISTRACTION BY OUR DREADED LORD BAALIKAR!
SURRENDER THE SECRETS OF THE CHRYSALIS TO ME!
RRUMBLE
OR FACE YOUR ANNIHILATION!
TOMORROW THERE WILL BE NOTHING LEFT TO FIGHT FOR.
RRUMBLE

WATCH OUT FOR PAPERCUTZ

Welcome to the fear-fraught fourth THE ONLY LIVING BOY graphic novel, by David Gallaher and Steve Ellis, from Papercutz – those patchwork people dedicated to publishing great graphic novels for all ages. I'm Jim Salicrup, Editor-in-Chief and the only living fanboy working at 160 Broadway on wintery weekends, here to offer up a poem...

Yes, I said "a poem"! I know I usually use my "My Watch Out for Papercutz" column to bring you up-to-date on the latest Papercutz news, but you can always check out papercutz.com for that. I'm resorting to publishing poetry because of Erik Farrell's current dire situation. I mean, after what's happened to the poor kid in THE ONLY LIVING BOY #3, I would totally understand if he just wanted to find a bed to hide in under the blankets for a year or so. Not that that would've made an especially exciting graphic novel! But Erik is something special. Like the watches in the long ago advertising slogan for Timex, Erik can take a beating and keep on ticking.

I know none any of us have been in exactly the predicament Erik's in now, but I'm sure we've all had to deal with major problems at some point. Who hasn't ever felt lost? Or felt that everything wasn't going your way? I think we all do at various times, especially when we've had to deal with seriously unpleasant things. I deal with it by trying to embrace all the positive things in my life–family, friends, comics, music, movies, etc. – and to remember this corny old poem by Frank Lebby Stanton (1857-1927) that I'd like to share with you now. It's called...

Keep A-Goin'
by Frank L. Stanton

If you strike a thorn or rose,
Keep a-goin'!
If it hails or if it snows,
Keep a-goin'!
'Taint no use to sit an' whine
When the fish ain't on your line;
Bait your hook an' keep a-tryin'--
Keep a-goin'!

When the weather kills your crop,
Keep a-goin'!
Though 'tis work to reach the top,
Keep a-goin'!
S'pose you're out o' ev'ry dime,
Gittin' broke ain't any crime;
Tell the world you're feelin' prime--
Keep a-goin'!

When it looks like all is up,
Keep a-goin'!
Drain the sweetness from the cup,
Keep a-goin'!
See the wild birds on the wing,
Hear the bells that sweetly ring,
When you feel like singin', sing--
Keep a-goin'!

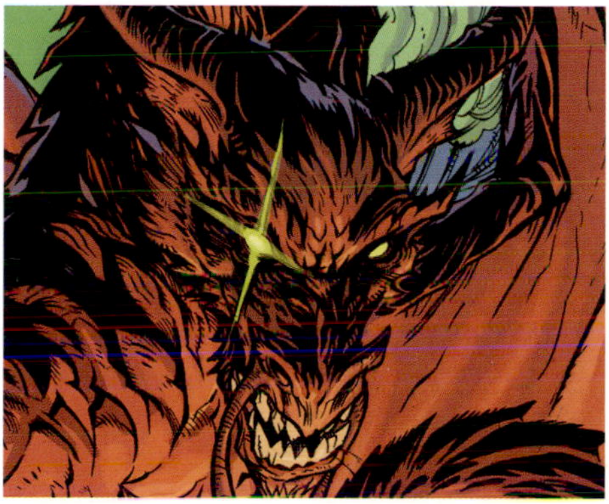

And that's what Erik does in this graphic novel, and that reminds me of the adage, "Be careful what you wish for..." because in THE ONLY LIVING BOY #5, Erik's confrontation with the mind-boggling, super-powerful Baalikar continues, and we can only hope that the only living boy can continue to keep on living! Be there for "To Save a Shattered World," Erik can use all the support he can get!

Thanks, and keep a-goin', Jim

STAY IN TOUCH!

EMAIL:	salicrup@papercutz.com
WEB:	papercutz.com
TWITTER:	@papercutzgn
FACEBOOK:	PAPERCUTZGRAPHICNOVELS
FAN MAIL:	Papercutz, 160 Broadway, Suite 700, East Wing, New York, NY 10038